Ellis Peters has gained u..............................
novels, and in particular for *The Chronicles of Brother Cadfael*, now into their eighteenth volume.

Also by Ellis Peters

The Chronicles of Brother Cadfael
A Rare Benedictine
Mourning Raga
Death to the Landlords
City of Gold and Shadows
Funeral of Figaro
Death Mask
Piper on the Mountain
Flight of a Witch
The Will and the Deed
The Horn of Roland

.

And writing as Edith Pargeter

The Brothers of Gwynedd Quartet
The Eighth Champion of Christendom
Reluctant Odyssey
Warfare Accomplished
She Goes to War
A Bloody Field by Shrewsbury

The Assize of the Dying

Ellis Peters

HEADLINE

Copyright © 1958 Edith Pargeter

The right of Ellis Peters to be identified as the Author of
the Work has been asserted by her in accordance with the
Copyright, Designs and Patents Act 1988.

First published in 1958
by William Heinemann Ltd

First published in paperback in 1991
by HEADLINE BOOK PUBLISHING

10 9 8 7 6 5 4

ISBN 0 7472 3645 3

Typeset in 10/12¼ pt Times
by Colset Private Limited, Singapore

Printed and bound in Great Britain by
Cox & Wyman Ltd, Reading, Berkshire

HEADLINE BOOK PUBLISHING
A division of Hodder Headline PLC
338 Euston Road
London NW1 3BH

CONTENTS

THE ASSIZE
OF THE DYING

Into the well of intense silence Mr Justice Manton let fall, in his beautiful, dispassionate voice: 'Do you find the prisoner at the bar guilty or not guilty of murder?'

The foreman of the jury, a highly strung little middle-aged architect, stood gripping the front of the box as though he were being asked to pronounce upon his own life and death, so desperately oppressed by the weight of history upon his inoffensive neck that his balding, fawn-coloured head trembled like a heavy flower upon an inadequate stem. In a dry croak he said: 'Guilty, my lord!' and it was upon his forehead, not the prisoner's, that an instant sweat broke out before the sound of the words had ceased.

Charlie's hand clenched for a moment upon Margaret's in a convulsion of pure excitement. She heard a sound like an enormous sigh that emanated from every corner of the crowded court, and realised that she had been holding her breath in the unbearable tension of waiting for that verdict, and that hundreds of other people must have been doing the same. There was more in the suddenly released sound than awe and pity: a horrid suggestion, to her ear, of sensuous enjoyment. After all, they were not responsible for the prisoner's plight; there was no reason why they should not get a legitimate thrill out of it. Even Charlie, already tucking his notes and pencil away one-handed in preparation for a quick departure to the nearest phone, could not quite keep the hiss of satisfied appetite out of his deep sigh. Then, as if he sensed her disapproval, he flashed a soft, placating glance along his shoulder at her, and made a deprecating grimace before he turned his eyes again upon the solitary grey figure standing in the dock.

Mr Justice Manton said, with the same immovable courtesy: 'Louis Bretherton Stevenson, you have been found guilty of the wilful murder of Zoë Trevor, at Hampstead, on the third of September last. Have you anything to say before sentence is passed upon you?'

The prisoner raised his shaggy grey head, and levelled the hollow brilliance of his ageing eyes upon the Judge's face. In this situation Margaret found him an incredible figure. He did not belong here at all; he belonged in the reading-room of the British Museum, or the chair of archæology at some obscure university, or to some byway of lost literature in which he could explore and write for ever without causing a ripple upon the oblivious surface of his century. He was tall, thin and slightly stooped, with all the marks of the scholar about him, and throughout the four days of the trial she had watched the public nature of his ordeal invade him gradually like a corrosive poison, dislocating his armour of habit joint by joint, and one by one upsetting every equilibrium he had perfected in his fifty-five years of highly personal living. Even if they had not found him guilty at the end of it, she thought bitterly, there would have been no way in the world of restoring him to his old condition. In a way, they'd already killed him: it only remained to regularise the position.

'Yes, my lord,' said Louis Stevenson, 'I have.'

His voice was quiet but clear, much as it must have sounded in the days when he had lectured at his provincial university, and periodically scandalised the faculty, as the prosecution had not failed to bring out, by the irregularities of his private life. There was nothing scandalous left in him now; he looked dusty and disorganised, shrunken into a smaller compass because of the necessity of preserving himself from the touch of a curiosity which nevertheless pursued him inch by inch even into his own body.

Mr Justice Manton waited, with his granite calm and patience unshaken. One elderly professional greyness confronted another. They might have been the two halves of a schizophrenic personality examining each other, on one side with uninhibited detestation, on the other with a cold tolerance at least as terrible. Margaret thought, with a sense of inevitability: 'Uncle John disliked him from the first moment he set eyes on him – I could see it. I suppose order always feels like that about disorder. But then, oughtn't he to have found some way of getting rid of the case? Or has he been pushing himself to the limit of fairness the other way, for fear of injustice?' For the Judge was incorruptibility in one man, and had been in the game so long that he was on guard against every motion of his own mind, and had subdued the impulses of his heart as an expert breaks a horse.

Supposing, of course, that he had a heart! But for the existence of her cousin Charlie, who was unquestionably his child, she would have found it difficult to believe that her uncle belonged to the same warm and fallible species as other men.

'I did not kill Zoë Trevor,' said the prisoner's muted but bitterly clear voice, 'but you, in the name of society, are about to kill me. To kill unjustly is murder, and since I have no remedy here I must and I do appeal for redress in another place.'

When he paused for an instant, as he did now, the weight and quality of the silence became intense. He was so far apart from the collective experience of this courtroom full of people that they could hardly comprehend what he was saying; and what was to come was something beyond their power to guess. They hung upon the faint greyish lips, and held their breath, avid for his alien flavour.

'I therefore summon the representatives of your guilt,' said Louis Stevenson, sweeping his disorientated glance suddenly round the court before he fixed again upon the Judge's impassive face, 'to answer for my murder. You, who have conducted the case against me—'

Counsel for the Prosecution gazed out from under his vast white brow and his unbecoming wig with a faintly embarrassed calm, as though he had accidentally overheard his distinguished name mentioned in a public place. Mr Justice Manton maintained his monolithic stillness, and waited for the protest to end. It was, after all, only a variation on all the other protests he had heard in similar circumstances in his long career.

'You, who pronounced the verdict of guilty against me—'

The foreman of the jury jumped as though a ghost had

nudged his arm, and wilted a little more grievously in his own heat. His mouth hung open and trembling.

'You, who summed up against me, and are about to condemn me to death—' The two pairs of fierce old eyes locked again, and this time the fixed stare held – 'and the man, whoever he may be, who committed the crime for which I am being killed. You four,' said Louis Stevenson, suddenly loud and peremptory through the stupefied quietness, 'I summon to meet me at the time appointed, at the Assize of the Dying.'

After his voice had ceased, the silence fell like a stone. No one understood, yet they felt, chillingly through the alien syllables, the conviction that they had been listening to an indictment. The words had to do with them all, and with the four he had selected in particular, and all they knew was that they were being threatened, and did not know from which quarter to expect the blow. They came out of their superstitious stillness with a rustle and a murmur, whispering to their neighbours in overwrought, shrill sibilants that mounted in a few seconds to a formidable crescendo of uneasiness. Here and there about the crowded court began the helpless, infectious giggles of hysteria. The reporters, stirring quickly out of their paralysis, were already on their marks like runners, waiting for release.

Mr Justice Manton lifted his head imperiously, and said: 'Silence!' in a knife-like voice that lopped off all sound far more effectively than the rapping of the gavel.

Charlie, his fingers pressing hard into Margaret's arm, whispered: 'But, my God, what does it *mean*? There's the one man who could tell us, and I bet you my old man won't ask him!' All the newspaperman in Charlie was quivering with curiosity and exasperation, to think that the Judge would pass by so intriguing an opening without exploring it. He knew his father very accurately; the measured voice, coldly courteous still, was merely asking gently:

'That is all you wish to say?'

'It is all, my lord. You'll find it enough.'

The Judge waited, erect, for the black cap to settle like a crow upon the curls of his wig. He began to pass sentence. Margaret pressed her shoulder against Charlie's arm, dropped her glance into her gloved palms and wished not to hear, but the stale, oppressive hush let the words fall upon her heavily one by one, and she could not avoid them.

'—and may the Lord have mercy on your soul.'

'And on yours, my lord!' said Louis Stevenson very softly, staring across the court from hollow, exhausted eyes. He was still looking back over his shoulder when they touched him on both arms, and he turned and went away with them, down slowly from view into the earth. They had killed him; they buried him.

She opened her eyes, which she had instinctively closed upon his going, and saw the court clearing like snow in the sun, the pressmen bolting for their telephones as soon as the Judge's stately back had vanished. The murmur had broken out again, was rising steadily to a high-pitched thrumming like angry bees, the outcry of gratified excitement. She felt for Charlie's sleeve as her eyes opened, and said aloud: 'But he didn't do it, you know!'

It was not Charlie's face she saw when she turned her head, nor Charlie's voice that answered readily: 'No, I don't think he did, either.'

She ought to have known that Charlie would be away ahead of the others, with his self-reliant memory already arranging impressions, and his fluent tongue composing the sentences which would roll over the wire to his paper already formed and finished. Probably he had even for-mulated by this time an inspired guess at the significance of the Assize of the Dying, and was busy talking his news editor into staking his reputation upon its accuracy. He might as well. Charlie had a flair which seldom failed him. And from the telephone he would fly to some mine of information, human or encyclopædic, to confirm his guess.

'We seem to be the only two people of our opinion,' said the unknown young man.

She had risen and moved to let him pass, with a quick, indifferent smile, but he seemed in no hurry to go. He was taller and broader than Charlie, with a darkly handsome face and extremely direct and candid eyes. Since he made no move to pass by, and they were holding up other peo-ple, she led the way into the gangway, where the stream of excited sensation-hunters was now thinning. The young man walked at her shoulder. His clothes, which were quiet and good, nevertheless had, she thought, a cut which was not quite native. His preoccupied frown, which had light-ened for a moment at the recognition of a doubt the fellow to his own, settled again upon straight, bold, dark brows.

'You don't mind my taking advantage of your open comment? It was like having the thought taken out of my mind.'

'It was rather like starting up an echo, too. One always likes to find one isn't entirely alone.'

'Would you mind telling me *why* you think he's innocent?'

'I'd tell you if I knew,' said Margaret, breathing in deeply the cold outer air as they came into the doorway. 'I just believe his version, I suppose. The devil of it is that I never meant to get involved in this business of believing or disbelieving. I came here only to see my uncle trying a case. I wanted to know something about him, after living with him for three years and never learning a thing. But I'm no wiser now than I was before.' She met the surprised gaze of the uncompromising eyes, and explained with a rueful smile: 'My name's Margaret Manton. I'm the Judge's niece.'

'That's a queer coincidence,' he said slowly. 'I came here to try to get to know somebody, too. I never had much chance when she was alive – I'm Canadian, I only arrived here about a week before she was killed, and I never saw her but once. My name's Malachi Rouault. I'm Zoë Trevor's cousin, and since she didn't make a will, and hadn't any nearer kin – well, they tell me I'm also her heir.'

They had tea together in a café in a back street. Why not? She had no wish to go home to the Judge's house in the leafy recesses of Clevely Square, where as yet there would certainly be no Charlie to lighten her unaccustomed anxiety and depression. She was used to selecting her own companions, making up her own mind about them with firmness and bearing with equanimity such mistakes as she made in the process; and instinctively she liked Malachi Rouault. Believing in the innocence of a condemned man could be, she found, a strong bond. They felt close, and alone, islanded unhappily from the thousands of Londoners who would devour the sensational headlines that evening with no feeling of being involved.

'I don't wonder at the verdict,' said Malachi, 'when you consider the circumstances. Two people living next door to each other in a quiet Hampstead road, a fairly wealthy and rather too well-known actress like Zoë, and a worn-out, disreputable old don like him, up to his eyes in debt, and all his old welcomes worn out long ago. Then *she* is found strangled one morning when her maid arrives, all her jewellery and whatever cash was in the house has vanished, and *his* finger-prints are all over her living-room, and not another to be found anywhere but those belonging to the house. Then he's found to have a necklace of hers tucked away in his own place. What else could they possibly think, except that he'd killed her?'

'And yet he didn't,' said Margaret doggedly.

'I know he didn't, but I know it in the teeth of the evidence. And then, the story he told – he's been on friendly terms with her, he says, for years; they enjoyed each other's company, and he was in and out of her place regularly in the evenings. If he was in the way, she told him so and he left, and no hard feelings. Who's going to believe in a relationship like that? Zoë, let's face it, had men running after her in their dozens from the time she was seventeen, according to all the evidence, but she seldom wasted her time on the old, unattractive and defeated. Then beyond that, if you believe him, you've got to believe that he went to see her that night and told her he was desperate for money, and she gave him – *gave* him! – the pearls to raise money to fend off his creditors.'

'I may be crazy,' said Margaret, 'but I do believe it. It's too tall to be anything but true – a lie would have been more plausible. And he told it from the beginning to the end, and nothing in it got changed. Have you ever had to tell a very complicated lie? The temptation to improve your case at every telling is irresistible. I can believe, too, that a man like that might be an acceptable companion to a woman like that, when she wanted none of the usual stresses, when she'd kicked off her shoes and let down her hair. Things do emerge about Zoë, you know, if you take his word for it. She was intelligent and well-read, she was real and she was generous.'

'You sound like half the argument I've been having with myself,' he said. 'If you believe that, you believe the rest of his story?'

'That she was expecting someone else for dinner? Yes, I believe it. I don't care if there was no trace of another visitor, there'd been plenty of time to remove the evidence. If there'd been servants living in, it would have been different, but whoever it was had all night to set his scene. And the dress she was wearing – changing it was more than he cared to tackle, I expect – that agrees very well with Stevenson's story that she was expecting a very special guest. It was rather a special toilette. Of course there were no other finger-prints – whoever came to dine with her didn't intend that there should be. It's wonderful how you can watch your fingers if your life depends on it, and he had time to polish any doubtful surfaces afterwards. If Stevenson had gone there to kill and rob her, the room wouldn't have been littered with the marks of *his* fingers either. All the evidence against him was there simply *because* he was innocent.'

'It doesn't look as if that's going to help him,' said Malachi moodily. 'I suppose he'll appeal.' But he sounded, she thought, exceedingly dubious about it, as though he had shared her impression that Stevenson was, in some obscure way, already a dead man, and beyond appealing against his fate. And that, in turn, reminded her only too well that he had appealed already, in full, clear terms, if only one knew the language.

'The papers will be blaring already,' she said, with a foreboding tremor. 'Can't you imagine the headlines? All the editors will be driving their staffs round from library to library, trying to find out what the Assize of the Dying is. And nobody will know.'

'*I* know!' said Malachi, raising his dark eyes suddenly to her face. The pupils appeared to her, seen thus closely across the table, as quite black, and the lashes, startlingly long and luxuriant in so decidedly masculine a face, darkened even the irises to a royal purple in their shadow. His smile, too, which came readily in answer to her look of astonishment and eagerness, had a womanish delicacy and subtlety, recalling the obvious French ancestry of his name.

'You *know*?' She locked her fingers together suddenly, aware of a desire to retreat from too close an understanding of the issues involved in Louis Stevenson's tragedy, but knowing that she had no intention of turning back. 'What is it?'

The melting Mediterranean eyes stared unwaveringly

13

into hers. 'I know I look more like a lumberjack, I'm sorry if you're disappointed – I teach, and my subject happens to be European literature. A thoroughly sedentary type!' He smiled, again with that extraordinarily gracious effect. 'You don't, by any chance, read the Spanish romances yourself? A lot of them have been trans-lated – not always very well. No? So you don't know the story of Count Alarcos. Well – this happens about the fourteenth century. A certain Count Alarcos was secretly betrothed to the Infanta of Spain, and then fell in love with another girl and took advantage of the secrecy to des-ert the Infanta and marry his new fancy. The Princess nursed her vengeance for some years, until the Count felt safe and happy in his marriage and had three children; then she told the whole story to the King, and demanded that Count Alarcos should kill his wife and marry her, to atone for the injury to his and her honour. His alternative was a traitor's death for himself. He couldn't take it. He went home, confessed to his innocent wife and told her to prepare for death. When she found he was quite deter-mined to clean his escutcheon, not to mention saving his life, by murdering her, she laid on him, the Infanta and the King her summons to the Assize of the Dying. People did, you know – quite often, when they had no other court of appeal. He strangled her with a scarf, and the curse took effect from that moment. The summons had to be answered within thirty days. The place—' His broad shoulders lifted resignedly. 'Well, what would you expect? There was only one court she could really trust to do her justice. The place was the judgement seat of God.'

'Then, to get there—' Margaret's voice was an awed whisper.

'Yes, of course! The Infanta on the eleventh day, the King on the twentieth – and before the thirtieth, Count Alarcos. They all died. There was no other way of complying with the summons, naturally. They had to die – that's what the Assize of the Dying meant.'

Margaret sat behind the tea-cups, surrounded by the shoddy gilt and fake marble of a cheap London café, and felt the comfortable scepticism of the age dissolving about her before a cold wind of credulity. 'But you tell it almost as if you believed in it!' she cried, pushing the possibility away from her.

'Believed in which, the belief or its effectiveness? I believe in the belief, of course, the evidence is plentiful enough. And in its effectiveness – well, people died of it. Does it make much difference whether they died because there was really a compulsion on them to die and keep their appointment, or because they believed in the thing and suggested themselves into a decline out of despair and resignation? In either case,' he said simply, 'wasn't the curse equally effective?'

'But it's fantastic! This is the twentieth century—'

He smiled. 'So they said, I understand, when they caught a coelacanth alive.'

'You don't seriously mean that you expect my uncle, and Sir Robert Wyvern, and the foreman of the jury, and some unknown person, to fall dead in the street?'

'I don't expect anything – except that once this story is in the headlines – and it probably is by now – London will be seething with such a hysterical sort of excitement that the accumulation of emotion might well be enough to blow a few people off the earth. In an atmosphere like

15

that, would it be so very surprising if somebody's nerve gave, and he auto-suggested himself into dying?'

'They may not find out,' said Margaret, clutching at a hope which felt precarious in her hand.

'It isn't as abstruse as all that. They'll find out soon enough. Your uncle,' said Malachi, smiling a little wryly, 'looks durable enough, but they can't all be granite. And then, you see, it needs only some quite harmless, ignorant person to pass out in the Underground with heart failure, and they'll have him for the real murderer – because that's what makes it so beautifully universal, no one knows who he is. No, the only way of saving everybody else, as far as I can see, is by saving Stevenson. By finding out who really killed my cousin Zoë, and proving it on him beyond doubt.'

Margaret raised her wide eyes, which were as blue as gentians and, by this subdued indoor light, as dark. 'You're absolutely sure that Stevenson is innocent?'

'Absolutely sure. Circumstantial evidence can prove what it likes, I prefer the evidence of my own senses. Stevenson laid a particularly awful curse on the man who killed Zoë and got him into this mess. And – surely you could see it yourself? – whoever doesn't believe in the Assize of the Dying, *Stevenson does*.'

It was just half-past five, and the traffic rush was in its full frenzy, when they walked to the corner of the street together. She had declined a taxi, and elected to walk through the park. Dusk was falling mistily over the din and flashing of the street, and the late evening editions were on the pavements. They heard, for once, a distinguishable cry from the doorway of the tube station, and started and drew closer together at the prophetic scream:

'Murder verdict sensation! Assize of the Dying – four people condemned!'

'You were right,' said Margaret. 'They've got it already. Now what happens?'

'Now everybody watches his neighbour, and wonders if he's the fourth man. Unless somebody can find out who *is*, in time to get Stevenson off.'

'I believe you feel as involved as I do,' she said, looking up into his face as they walked side by side, alone on pavements where thousands of anonymous others were rushing hither and thither round them.

'She was my cousin. And don't forget, what she left comes to me. I'm involved whether I like it or not.'

'But if the police didn't find out anything, what can we do?' The 'we' came naturally, and was not even noticed. 'Where can we even begin, after all this time?'

Malachi said, taking her arm instinctively as they halted at the edge of the pavement to wait for the lights to change: 'I got the key of her house today – the house in Hampstead, where it happened. I'm going up there tomorrow to have a look at the place. I don't know where else to start. Probably there's nothing to find there, and not much anywhere else. But I've got to try.'

'I should like to come with you,' she said.

They forgot about the lights, and the released surge of people across the street left them still standing there, gazing at each other, trying to see more than there was to be seen in a human face, trying to drag years of understanding out of a mere moment of feeling.

'Of course!' said Malachi very slowly and quietly. 'If

17

you're sure you don't want to turn back now, while there's time.'

'I'm sure.'

He took her arm again, suddenly moving with a new abruptness, as if she had pointed out his direction to him, and reassured him that it led somewhere definite. 'Come on, let's get out of this din. We can talk better in the park.'

But the orange light was already bright again in the dusk, and as they turned to cross on the heels of the scuttling crowd the red winked into life. They checked resignedly as the wave of cars shot forward. A little drab, darting figure jostled them at the last moment and made off across the road at a practised run, head down, abstracted and frowning inwardly upon his own private worries even under the wheels of the traffic. A middle-aged man in a fawn raincoat and a bowler hat, spectacled, running like a whippet and still dignified – something you could see a dozen times a day in London, thought Margaret, watching him with a sudden impulse of laughter. The cars checked and shrieked indignantly in the act of bounding forward, withheld their weight just long enough to let him spring clear. A heavy van resignedly hesitated, poised like a ballerina, and swooped forward on his heels.

It was at that instant that the frog-voiced newsboy on the pavement opposite shook out under the lamp his brand-new red-and-white poster that shrieked: 'Assize of the Dying!' in letters eight inches high, and gave tongue triumphantly to match the mammoth type, with a bellow of: 'Sensation! Four people to die! Four people to die!'

*   *   *

What happened was over in a moment, and yet it seemed to Margaret as deliberate and balletic as a slowed-up section of film. The running man, hit in the face by the shout and the scare-type together, leaped out of his abstraction with a quivering start, and hung for an instant incredibly still, apparently in mid-air. The brakes of the nearest car screamed; the tension broke and bore him not forward but backward, under the wing of the van, which was in the act of accelerating to draw clear. Spun round by the blow, he faced them for a fraction of a second under the lamplight, his bowler gone, his thin, lank fringes of hair flung erect, his face a recognisable mask of terror. Then the van was braking too late, voices were screaming with a knife-edged sound, and under the wheels a brownish bundle was dragged limply over and over along the blackly shining street.

Margaret had not uttered a sound. Malachi took her forcibly by the shoulders and pulled her round breast to breast with him, and when she instinctively turned her head to gaze back at the horrid knot of men and vehicles in the middle of the street he seized her by the chin and jerked her face round to him again, not even gently.

'Don't look! Here, come away! There's nothing we can do, they've got more than enough witnesses here.'

He shut his arm round her hard, and drew her away along the street until the queer clamour and queerer succeeding quietness fell behind. She was trembling, but silent. As soon as she was forced to move she had control of her body again; she shook off his constricting arm, and walked beside him steadily.

It was he who halted, as soon as they were too far away

to see anything. He drew her to the shop windows, and said in a strained voice: 'Will you wait for me here? And not come after me? I've got to be sure.'

'You are sure,' said Margaret, lifting to him eyes dilated and fixed with horror. 'You saw his face when he was hit. So did I. We couldn't be mistaken, not both of us.'

'That isn't what I meant. I just have to find out if – how badly he's hurt.'

She had never been more sure of anything in her life than that the little man was dead, but she consented to wait with resignation while Malachi went back to make more certain of certainty. When he came back to her his face was arduously blank and quiet, but the level of his voice was too brittle to be convincing. 'Come on, let's get out of this. The ambulance is there already. They didn't lose any time.'

'He's dead, isn't he?' said Margaret, flattening her cold palms unsteadily against the plate-glass window at her back. He tried to take her arm and lead her gently away, to avoid the far too intimate and naked meeting of eyes in which stillness immediately involved them, but she resisted the persuasion of his hand at her elbow, and suddenly took him by the lapels and held him facing her, insisting in a whisper: 'He *is* dead – isn't he?'

'It was his own fault, he lost his head. He – the van went over him. Yes – he's dead.'

He felt her trembling, though the motionless calm of her face was not shaken. He shut her body between his big hands to steady her, and was astonished by her slightness. It was like holding a child. He did not want to look into her eyes, because she would only see in his the

20

reflection of what she was thinking, and it would be far better for her if she could forget it; but now her face seemed all eyes, and there was nowhere else to look.

'And it *was* him – wasn't it? We didn't make a mistake? We didn't imagine it?'

'We didn't imagine it,' he said, in what was almost a groan. 'It's the foreman of the jury.'

By the time she let herself into her uncle's house in Clevely Square she had regained her balance, and was repeating to herself all the sensible arguments Malachi had poured into her ears during the walk through the park. There was nothing supernatural about the death, it was a simple case of over-wrought nerves giving way at a dangerous moment, and causing a perfectly understandable accident. The case, in a manner of speaking, had certainly been the cause of the lapse, but not for any esoteric reasons. And most convincing of all, as Malachi had reminded her, not even the most credulous could attribute the disaster to the Assize of the Dying, since that would take effect only when Louis Stevenson was dead, supposing that there was anything in it at all; and Louis Stevenson had all the resources of appeal left to him yet before he need resign himself to dying.

The shock had left her exhausted, but she had control of herself now, and could look at the thing reasonably. All the same, she lost no time in looking for her uncle. The accident was scarcely news at all until its connection with the Stevenson case dawned upon the pressmen, and in any case it had happened too late for the last editions tonight, so the Judge could not yet have heard of it. She was not sure why she felt bound to report it to him so promptly; it was as though he were entitled to know all the developments in the case, in order to protect himself. And yet she did not believe in it!

He was in the library, sitting over a fire with the late evening papers. Without his wig, and in slippers and spectacles, he did not appear to her much more approachable than in court, with all the weight of the law in the lift of his ascetic fingers. The long, clear, fastidious profile against the flames had a forbidding beauty, the carriage of the shoulders and head was as upright as a guardsman's. Wherever you looked at him, however you approached him, he had no weaknesses. She thought that was why she had never been able to feel anything warmer than respect for him. Charlie was all his mother, according to the accounts Margaret had heard of that enchanting and lamented lady: unpredictable, fallible, human, insubordinate, prepared to attempt anything for a dare. It was so easy to go and pluck Charlie by the arm, and pour out to him anything that might be on your mind; nothing could daunt him and few things astonished him. But this just and immovable being was quite another matter.

He looked up when she entered, and met her with his grave smile. 'Why, Margaret, my dear, I was wondering where you were.'

'I was in court this afternoon,' said Margaret. She went and knelt on the rug to tease the fire into a brighter blaze. 'I met somebody and had tea with him afterwards, or I should have been back before. But what I wanted to tell you was that something happened on the way home—'

Mr Justice Manton folded the newspaper meticulously while he listened to her, without interruption, with all the attentive courtesy he had extended to Louis Stevenson before sentencing him to death. Then he said, but more clearly and decisively, all the sensible things Malachi had said before him. All but the last. She could not see that the additional death had moved him in the least, because it was a part of his ethical equipment, as a judge, to resist being moved either back or forth by emotional considerations. Even his feelings were incorruptible.

'I know all that! And then, of course,' she said, with a sigh, 'they can hardly even make out that there's anything supernatural about it, I suppose, while Stevenson is still alive. The curse could hardly be supposed to take effect until he died, could it?' She rose, shaking out her skirts sadly. The old eyes were watching her with a remote and intent gentleness.

'I should not attach any importance to that idea, either, if I were you, my dear. The poor fellow's death was simply a regrettable accident, caused by his – I'm afraid – too impressionable nature. It has no other connection whatever with the Stevenson case. Put the idea out of your head.'

'What matters isn't what goes on in my head, but what the public are going to make out of it,' said Margaret sharply. 'Telling them to forget it isn't going to be very effective. If it weren't for the fact that Louis Stevenson is still alive, there'd be a fine orgy of hysteria starting up by morning, when this affair hits the headlines—'

The curious, rueful fixity of his gaze stopped her. He was holding out to her the paper he had been reading.

'What is it? What's the matter?'

23

She took the paper slowly. A long forefinger touched the blurred red type of the stop-press item, the only one, askew in its column. It was brief enough:

STEVENSON COMMITS SUICIDE

Louis Stevenson, sentenced to death this afternoon for the murder of Zoë Trevor, was found to have severed an artery on his way back to prison after sentence, and died in the prison hospital shortly after half-past five this evening.

It is not known how he obtained the instrument used, which is thought to have been a worn-down metal plate from a shoe.

Half-past five! Staring at the blank space beneath the smeared red type, Margaret saw again, with peculiar clarity, the round, confident face of the jeweller's clock at which she had stared steadily all the time she was waiting for Malachi to bring her the news she already knew. When he had left her there, it had stood at twenty-one minutes to six, and already some three or four minutes had passed since the traffic had screamed to a stand-still. Between death and death, between the crime and the first act of redress – how many minutes? Five?

'This is the room where the maid found her body,' said Malachi. 'Nothing's been moved since, except that they took away both the cushions from the ends of the settee. This one, nearer the door, was torn by the buckle of her shoe, so they told me. *That* one, where her head was, was stained with a drop or two of blood from the lobe of her ear. Her ear-clips – well, they must have been pulled off in a hurry – before—'

'Before she was quite dead,' said Margaret, relieving him of the words he baulked at saying.

'Well – yes. She'd been reading, they said; the book was turned down quite neatly on the floor by the settee, the way you might put down some not very important novel when somebody came in.'

'As somebody did come in. Somebody she knew, or she'd have abandoned her book in a very different fashion. Somebody she was expecting.'

'That was considered as strong a point against Stevenson as for him, if you remember.'

'Does that matter to us?' asked Margaret. 'We know he was innocent.' Somehow the past tense had also removed all the conditions from that knowledge.

'Yes. We know it, but we're too late to save him.'

She said in a low voice: 'I think we always were. In a way he was murdered when they arrested him. But we might save something for him. He still has a right to justice. We can't stop now.'

'No,' he agreed soberly, 'we can't stop now.'

To this point all conversation led this morning. Louis Stevenson's resolute exit from a world which used him so ill had not made the pursuit of truth unnecessary, but only more urgent. The issue had become something much bigger than just one man, and they could not stop now.

'She was lying here on the settee with her book,' said Margaret, sitting down there slowly where Zoë Trevor had reclined that night for the last time. 'He said she had the table beautifully laid for two in the next room, and she was watching the door expectantly when he left her. The man who came in must have been the man she expected. When did the doctors say she must have died?'

'Between seven-thirty and ten in the evening. But they seemed to think it likely it was somewhere in the middle of that period.'

'The middle of an early September evening, after a lovely day. The windows would be open.' She got up restlessly and went to the wide window, outside which the trees of the garden, now leafless, spread at a little distance their delicate bony hands. Beyond these filigree screens she could see glimpses of the reddish levels of tennis courts. 'That's the club grounds, isn't it? In late summer no one would be able to see in here, but leaves wouldn't keep sounds from getting in and out. If she'd screamed, somebody would have heard her. It's no distance to those courts, and on a fine evening at the end of summer there'd be somebody playing as long as the light lasted.'

'They never found anyone who had heard anything,' said Malachi, coming to her shoulder and gazing out with her at the grey skies and the bare olive-green of the hedges.

'Then there never was anything to hear.' She turned, and stood looking in silence for a long time at the settee on which Zoë's beautiful dead body had lain, as elegant as in sleep except that she had drawn up her knees at the assault of the hands about her neck, and slashed across the silk of the cushion at her feet with the ornate buckle of one shoe. There had been no cry, and no fight for her life. Why not? It takes only an instant to shriek aloud, not more than a couple of seconds to bound to the open window and send a shout echoing unmistakably across the garden to the tennis courts beyond the hedge.

'Malachi, I don't understand at all. Granted a casual friend could have walked in on her here without startling her in the least, still he couldn't reach the point of touching her, of putting his hands round her neck, without making her aware that everything was wrong. If she got up from here to greet him – the man she expected – still she was quite at ease about his visit, and she went back to her place. And he was able to follow her, to lay hands on her, without frightening her – so that she never even had time, between realising and dying, to utter a sound. Until he actually tightened his hands round her throat, she never suspected anything was wrong. Do you see what it means?'

'Yes,' said Malachi. 'It means what the whole set-up of the dress and the dinner meant. It means a lover.'

'It couldn't be anyone else, could it?' Margaret laid her hand wonderingly where the bright, famous, heedless head had rested. 'And even then, I still wonder how he managed it. I should think she was a woman of quick reactions. Say he was here on the settee with her, his weight lying over her would keep her from struggling, his arms holding her would prevent her from breaking free or fighting him off. But even then there must have been a moment when she *knew*. Even if he had complete control of his face, there must have been a moment when the sense of his touch changed, when the hands went to her throat. But she never uttered a sound.'

'There might have been quite enough noise and chatter going on in the park to cover any sound she made.'

'There may, but it seems a risk for him to take. Look

at the distance! You could toss a pebble into the middle of that first court if the trees weren't there. Would he take a chance like that?'

'He was taking risks whatever he did.'

'Yes, but intelligently – because, you know, he didn't leave behind one touch, one hint, of his own personality. Nothing but this imaginative picture we've been making.' She reared her head back suddenly, lifting to his face her large, dedicated eyes, dark with an intent gravity. 'Malachi, this was a very single-minded soul – this murderer. I don't think anyone or anything outside the bounds of himself and his own interests was real to him. Do you remember the medical evidence well? I'd just be interested to know – did they say there were any facial injuries?'

Mystified, gazing at her with a curiously wary face, he replied slowly: 'They said there was extensive cyanosis, of course – and some local bruising of the lips. From the congestion of blood, I suppose – at least there didn't seem to be any traceable marks of fingers, except round the throat.'

'No,' said Margaret gently, 'not fingers. I'm beginning to know quite a lot about this man. I know now how he stopped her mouth, right up to the moment when he was quite safe and she had no breath any longer for crying out. It wasn't his fingers. It was his lips that were hard over hers. He was kissing her when he began to kill her.'

'A lover of Zoë's?' said Charlie, elevating his mobile eyebrows. 'My dear girl, that makes everything easy! Don't you realise that they come in their hundreds round

28

this town? You're faced with a selection from half the presentable men in London between, say, twenty-five and forty. A needle in a haystack presents much the same problem, I'm told. Let me get you another drink, Meg – what are you on?'

'No, thanks, I've had my allowance.'

'Rouault? Yes, do keep me company! Are you sticking to beer?' He came back with his own recharged glass and Malachi's tankard, and dropped again into his corner seat. For Charlie he was unusually grave; the slight, tender curl of the strongly marked lips was a smile of half-rueful reminiscence rather than amusement or gaiety. 'When I came out of the RAF in 1946 I was in a bad way for a bit. No more excitement, no more easy success, no more reliable thrills. Lucky me, I fell in with Zoë. There was all the excitement a man ever needed, and the success, if it wasn't easy, was extremely satisfying. I don't know how well you knew your cousin? No – well – she was out of her time, really. She belonged in the Italian Renaissance, or perhaps ancient Greece – she'd have made a superb *hetæra*. They don't come these days without a touch of the commercial, but Zoë hadn't any – not a drop of venal blood in her veins. She favoured you of her own personal will, or not at all. And when she went, she went without any asking leave.'

He met Malachi's measuring eyes, and shrugged and smiled. 'I was one of a long procession – a very small incident. She came to me from a poet, and left me for a painter. Come to think of it, if you really want to know how she looked in her heyday, you should go to Frank Franks. He painted and sketched her steadily for over a year, and as far as I know he kept all the best things he did of her. And if you're really serious about looking up all her old admirers, you could do worse than start with him. There's a man who had it very badly for Zoë – very badly indeed. But I told you, you're setting out to sift a whole generation.'

'I hardly think we need consider the wealthy ones—' began Margaret.

'What wealthy ones?' The hollow dimples dived inward in Charlie's long cheeks. 'Are you trying to tell me you're looking for some poor devil who loved Zoë, and is hard up for money? Which of us isn't? The poor girl doesn't give you much help, actually, does she? She made a lot of money herself, and threw it about like mad – she didn't care if the fellows she happened to like hadn't a bean. You'll find more than half her admirers live in a chronic state of brokeness, and most of the others just get by. Nobody's rich any more – not below the age of fifty, anyhow.'

'I've heard of this man Franks,' said Malachi thoughtfully. 'What is he? A successful Academy painter? I got the impression he was quite a fashionable man.'

'Oh, lord, no – strictly a Left Bank type. But yes, fashionable enough in his way. He does all right.'

'I've met him once or twice,' said Margaret. 'I think he'd remember me. We could go and see him.' Charlie watched them exchange understanding glances, and smiled his faintly wry, unquenchably merry smile. 'I never saw Zoë – I'm beginning to think it might be important,' said Margaret. 'Even if the best we can do now is a portrait.'

'It might, at that,' said Charlie softly, staring into his memory with the thoughtful tenderness back on his lips.

'But, listen, have you two seriously thought what you're doing?' He put Zoë away from him with a last lingering look of pleasure, and became as neatly practical as a new machine. 'The poor devil's dead! I never thought he'd go that way, I thought he was set to fight to the last ditch and I even thought he might win. And I'm sorry! But neither you nor anyone else can bring him back now.'

'No – we know that.' It was plain from Margaret's tone that she understood that this consideration should have made all the difference; and plainer still that in fact it made none.

'All right, you're going to put right what's been done wrong and set justice up again in her own esteem. I can sympathise with that. But all the same, I should think carefully what you're taking on, before you get too involved in this business to back out.'

'We won't drag you into it,' Margaret promised him with a preoccupied smile. 'I know you think he probably did it – that makes all the difference. But we're sure he didn't, and feeling like that, how can we let it alone? Especially as no one else is interested.'

Charlie spread his elbows across the table, and looked from one face to the other with a serious frown. 'That's exactly where you're wrong, and exactly what I'm pointing out. Someone else *is* interested, or will be, just as soon as you seem to be getting anywhere. Supposing, of course, that you're right, and Stevenson was innocent. Somebody's going to be very interested indeed, when you ferret out the first real line of inquiry.'

Her mind was hardly on what he was saying. She said indifferently: 'Oh, you mean the police!'

'I mean the murderer!' said Charlie.

31

* * *

Frank Franks had a studio in Chelsea, a Vandyke beard and a dedicated eye which exercised itself, all the while he talked with them, in the fierce, forceful shapes of light and shadow which composed Malachi's face, and the fascinating patterns of wintry sunlight in Margaret's hair, which was of a colour neither honeyed nor brown nor gold, but had its moments of being all three. They were not, for him, people, but arrangements of form and colour, and a dual and suspect curiosity was the only non-visual quality they had. He understood that Malachi's inheritance gave him a natural right to want to know the truth about Zoë's murder, but he had – they could be heard in his voice and seen in his every move-ment – reservations about the weight and urgency of such a curiosity as they displayed. For a cousin who had hardly known Zoë in her lifetime, this passionate con-cern seemed to him obsessive; and the girl was not even connected with the case at all.

He was, however, an artist, and allowed other people their obsessions if they respected his. He made them free of his studio, and produced for them a dozen sketches and two canvases. He had very little to say, and that was concerned far more closely with the formation of Zoë's body than the motions of her spirit. It was difficult to think of him as a lover.

The sketches, all but a couple of delicate decorations composed as much of drapery as of the woman within, were nude studies, spare and chaste and faceless. The smaller canvas was a woman asleep, relaxed as a cat, a magnificent arm flung up above the head, the face shad-owed by a great red-brown wave of hair, heavy and smooth as silk. The larger canvas he set up for them with a disdainful smile upon an easel, and turned it to the light for their inspection.

'This is more what you want. I kept it for two reasons, because it's unconscionably like her and by the time I finished it I no longer had the reality to look at – and because I was ashamed to sell it. My worst lapse, I call that. I did it to please her, but she had too much innate sense to be pleased with it, after all. Still, it's Zoë. If you want to know what she looked like, well, there she is.'

There she was indeed, in probably the nearest thing to a calculated Academy portrait he would ever paint, a half-length, seated against silver-grey curtains, in a picture frock of deep, soft blue, with a tightly swathed bodice and full, cascading skirt. From the foam of tulle the upper part of her body, naked-shouldered, grew like a vigorous flower, thrusting upward, erect and opulent towards the light, the head with its great heavy helmet of russet hair poised challengingly upon a throat long, rounded and full. The face had a splendid repose, assured and humorous and good-natured. It was easy to see how she might have afforded release to a great many young men disorientated by the transition from war to peace. There was room in that large presence to shake oneself free from all cramping fears that excitement was over.

'How could any man bear to kill her?' said Margaret, staring at the noble throat. 'It doesn't seem as if there could possibly be anything to gain that would pay for what he'd be losing.'

The painter shot her a darkly interested glance, and

agreed abruptly: 'It would certainly be like pulling down the house on top of himself.'

'She was really like that?'

'As sumptuous as that. Five foot five, and slender, but larger than life-size. And I made a magazine cover out of her! Look at the detail! My God, a new pre-Raphaelite tragedy! Every fold of the tulle is there – even the ear-clips you could pick out anywhere after seeing this. No wonder I suppressed it!'

The ear-clips, now that he mentioned them, were certainly painted with the precision of a miniaturist, and were worth looking at. Margaret had never seen any quite like them. They were of the exact blue of the dress, and, judging by their glitter, were composed of sapphires – single germander speedwell flowers, with a tiny leaf and stem of green enamel on silver; the preciosity of the painting was such that there was no mistaking the materials.

'She always wore those clips with that dress – I never saw them apart. They were a present from some fellow back in the days of her innocence.' He passed his fingertips over the encrustations of impasto with which he had achieved the glitter, and made a wry face. 'It's the dress she was wearing when they found her – I suppose you knew that?'

'I recognised it from the descriptions,' said Margaret, her eyes fixed darkly upon the shining drops, the same, it seemed, which had been ripped from Zoë's ear-lobes before the life was quite gone out of her. She pictured a hand, gloved now, turning the heavy head from one cheek to the other upon the cushion, plucking at the stones, leaving a minute drop or two of blood upon the silk under the shadow of the smooth hair. These, then, were the jewels which might still carry, somewhere in the infinitesimal hollows of their setting, traces of Zoë's blood.

She did not wonder that the really striking thing about the dress had not impressed itself upon the police mind, not upon Malachi's now. It was evidence for a woman, not a man. Nor did she point it out to him until they had taken their leave of Frank Franks, and were walking through a faint, silvery mist along the Embankment.

'Not much to be made out of that,' said Malachi ruefully, 'unless it's that he isn't by any means as single-minded about his art as he pretends. To hear him talk, she meant nothing to him but a set of values in light and form. But did you see his hand shake when he touched her? Do you suppose, after all, this could have been a crime of jealousy? It would be good cover to make it look like a sordid murder for theft – nothing could be much further from a *crime passionnel*, could it?'

Margaret shook her head. 'No, if that had been true, he might have taken some of the jewellery from her bedroom, but he wouldn't have made a clean sweep, even to the clips out of her ears. No, I'm sure of it, she was killed for what she'd fetch – somebody looked round for an easy source of income, to tide him over a crisis. And she came easy. Yes, even Zoë. Everybody's easy for somebody, it seems, and this man was Zoë's Achilles', heel. Usually they loved her, and she let herself be loved, but once, just once – the positions were reversed. This once, I'm sure, it wasn't Zoë who got bored and moved on, but the man. She must have loved him so much that even

after several years he had only to make the first move
of reconciliation, and she was ready to sweep everybody else out of her life to make room for him to come
back. That's why the little dinner *à deux*, that's why
the dress. Didn't you notice anything odd about the
dress?'

He was looking down at her, wide-eyed, a little
alarmed by the clairvoyant air she had in her absorption.
'No, I can't say I did. It was a very handsome one, of
course, but—'

'And the date of the painting, you didn't notice that? I
think I should have known even without the date, but
evening dresses don't change as drastically as all that,
and I suppose a man wouldn't see much wrong with it.
But he'd signed and dated the picture – it was finished in
May 1948. That means that on the night of her death she
was wearing a dress six years old. What an extraordinary
thing for Zoë to do!'

Malachi's face cleared, though his enlightened smile
was faintly sceptical of this crystal-gazing attitude
towards evidence. 'I see! So that's why you're deducing
that she wore it for a six-year-old love she'd unexpectedly recovered out of the past. A dress associated with
former happiness!'

'Why, unless it had a very special meaning for her,'
said Margaret simply, 'do you suppose a woman like Zoë
would even keep a dress as long as that? No, we needn't
bother any more about Zoë's recent affairs – it couldn't
have been any of them. The man we want is someone
from around the year 1948, someone from the heyday of
the blue dress.'

'Someone, in fact,' said Malachi, startled, 'from the

period of Frank Franks himself. Do you suppose that's why he was so casual – and so co-operative?'

Margaret was called to the telephone, late that evening, to hear with a shock of pleasure the expected voice. Malachi was himself, over the telephone, as firmly as he was in the flesh, though the transmission contrived to flatten a little the full tones of his voice, and made him sound more transatlantic than when she was in his presence. The most striking effect of this experience of hearing without seeing him was to put out of mind all the contradictory, womanish subtleties of liquid eyes and sensitive mouth, and make the iron part of him more apparent.

'Margaret? I didn't fetch you out of the bath, or anything? Are you alone?'

'You sound like a conspirator,' she said. 'But if it matters, I am alone. I've got something to tell you, too – not very much, but it just might mean something's moving. Who speaks first?'

'Go ahead! I can wait.'

'Well, I told you it wasn't so much. But Charlie told me this evening that they'd had a release from the police, too late for tonight's editions, that a small brooch, believed to be from Zoë's collection, had been found in a back-street pawnbroker's shop, somewhere in London. That was all they had. But it's something, isn't it? It's the first glimpse of a lead so far from the jewellery.'

'I rang you up to talk about the very same thing,' said Malachi, his voice sharpening into eagerness. 'For once I'm a jump ahead of Charlie. I had a visitor tonight, in fact he's only just left. A policeman! It seems they've been combing all the known fences in London ever since the case broke, and keeping an eye on all the shops that deal in second-hand jewellery. Routine stuff, it's been going on for months without any result until now. Yes, they've found a brooch. It's one of the least distinctive pieces that disappeared, in that nondescript style they're using these days for diamonds – I imagine that's why it was allowed to move on without being broken up, because I dare say you could duplicate this pretty easily around London. Evidently he didn't think it could be decisively identified as Zoë's, and maybe it wouldn't have, but for a peculiarity in the pin. It has a safety catch that sticks badly unless you get it in one exact position, and Zoë's maid has a good memory for things like that. The police just tried her on it, none too hopefully.'

'And she knew it? Positively?'

'She knew it, all right. Tilted it to the angle she remembered, opened it at once and without hesitation said: "That's hers!" '

'Then, Malachi – they know who took it to the shop?' Startled by the rising excitement of her own voice, she suppressed it hastily to a whisper. 'They haven't got the man, have they?'

'No luck! Not even a description that means anything.'

'But somebody in the shop must know how the brooch came there!'

Malachi laughed. 'He knows all right! I don't say he knows who the murderer is, because, after all, this thing may have come through a dozen pairs of hands since then. But he knows who brought the brooch to him, all right. Only he isn't saying! He says he bought it in good faith, from a man he didn't know and had never seen before, but who gave him a name and address, and seemed perfectly genuine. He supplied the name and address, but of course there's no such place and no such person. It seems the police have nothing positive on this pawnbroker fellow, though they have their suspicions about him. They incline to think that he must know the man who brought in the brooch, has probably disposed of pieces for him before, and only risked trying to sell the brooch as it stands because it was thought commonplace enough in appearance to get by. But they can't prove a word, and they haven't managed to get anything out of him that's going to help them much.'

'But if it's a question of keeping out of trouble himself—'

'He isn't in trouble. That's the beauty of it. There's not a thing they can charge against him, and won't be, unless he gets rattled and does something silly. And by all accounts, he won't.'

'But simply to cover himself, he must have given them some sort of account of the man from whom he had the brooch.'

'Oh, a detailed account, but not a word of it will be true, of course. A credible description, too! A man of middle age, gentleman, dressed well, but clothes much worn, light brown hair, thinning on top, moustache, military bearing, limp – the ex-officer finding it difficult to compete in the modern world, watching his standard of living go down the slides, and finally coming furtively and shamefacedly into a seedy little jeweller's to raise money on the first of his wife's trinkets. They tell me it's happening to more fixed-income people than you'd think. Even the false address makes sense in that picture. The police seemed to think it was quite an artistic performance on his part. But they don't believe for a minute that it's true, and neither do I.'

'Then we're no further forward than we were before,' said Margaret, her voice flat with disappointment.

'I wouldn't say that. Once a thread has appeared it must lead somewhere. Mightn't there be a possibility that the jeweller would talk a little more freely to somebody who *wasn't* the police? Supposing he wasn't involved himself – I mean in anything to do with the actual murder – mightn't he think it worthwhile picking up a bonus wherever he could find it? I've got a hunch that whatever he knew, he didn't know he was handling the product of a murder. A theft is one thing, but a murder's another. I'm told these respectable fences prefer to keep as far away from killers as they do from the police. Well, I'm neither. I might get on very well with him, on a purely business footing. It's worth trying, isn't it?'

'You mean you'd offer to pay for what he can tell you?' Margaret sounded doubtful, and for a moment even a little afraid.

'It's Zoë's money,' said Malachi sadly. 'Can you think of a better way to spend it?'

'No, I suppose you're right. When are you going to see him? Malachi, the police may be watching his moves.'

'I know. They'll have to see whatever they see, that's all. I would have gone tonight, but until I can get to a bank I've no cash – not the kind of cash he'd be interested in. I shall go tomorrow.'

'Can I come with you?' she asked simply.

'Why not? In broad daylight there can hardly be any risk attached.'

'Will you call me tomorrow, then?' She hesitated, frowning anxiously over the receiver. 'Malachi, there's one thing I don't really understand. The police – they don't think there's anything queer about *you*? Why should they send a man to tell *you* about this brooch being found? I mean, so promptly?'

A hollow and strangely unamused laugh echoed in her ear. 'You forget!' said Malachi. 'Along with all the rest of Zoë's belongings, the brooch is my property now.'

The back part of the shop was very dark, and the glimmer of the single electric bulb which burned over the counter soon fell behind them. The rich glow of semi-precious stones in the glass cases dimmed with it, the deep colours of amethyst and opal, unfashionable and sumptuous, gave place to a wilderness of miscellaneous junk, beads and bric-à-brac, filmed over thinly with dust.

It was the first time Margaret had ever seen the inside of a pawnbroker's shop. It came as a treacherous stab to her belief in the virtues of the present that such an establishment could still show an appearance of prosperity. Dustily and furtively, but with admirable confidence and calm, Mr Fredericks thrived and fattened. The rear shelves of the more withdrawn half of his business were full of pledges. Probably his touching portrait of the retired officer, giving a false name as he hawked his wife's jewellery, had been drawn entirely from life.

Mr Fredericks himself was short, thick-set and curiously rural in appearance, with a fresh complexion and an unabashed eye, but the stillness of the rosy face and the steel-bright steadiness of the light-grey eyes were urban accompaniments. Malachi's calculated candour, complete with names though not with motives, had made no more impact upon that imperturbable front than would the circuitous approach he might more reasonably have expected. He shook his head and made sympathetic noises about the premature death of Zoë Trevor. It had been a fearful shock to him when the police had suggested that the brooch was hers. No such idea had ever entered his head. Well, the thing had been exposed for sale openly on his counter, hadn't it? What better proof of good faith could a man offer?

'I tell you what, though, Mr Rouault,' he confided, leaning over the end of his counter until his face was very close to Malachi's, 'I can't believe that poor fellow who brought it in here ever did anything like that, I can't really. As pleasant a fellow as you could meet round the town these days, and it's my belief, if they ever do find him, they'll find there's more behind it, and he's being made use of by somebody else.'

'I'm pretty sure he is,' said Malachi, with a hollow smile. 'But I hardly think they ever will find him – do you?'

Mr Fredericks remained benign; indeed, the most notable thing about him was the quality of his serenity. Among much that was spurious and hardly bothered to cover its artificiality beyond the point of satisfying decency, his placidity was real enough. Whoever was suffering from qualms in the matter of the identity of a murderer, it was not Mr Fredericks. He was not afraid,

42

he was not even uneasy. He felt quite safe, because he knew nothing, or next to nothing, and was shrewdly happy in his ignorance and much too wise to jeopardise it with curiosity.

'*He* can't lead us to the man who did it,' thought Margaret, watching the encounter in silence, 'because he doesn't know who he is. The most he can do for us is put us one step on the way; and I believe he's almost certain already that, if he sells us that much help, it won't take us far. That's why he's so light-hearted about it.'

'I couldn't say, I'm sure,' said Mr Fredericks almost reproachfully, 'how good the police are at their job. I'm glad it's their business and not mine. I was always a very timid man. Not like you Canadians, Mr Rouault. I don't believe in asking for trouble.'

'Some people even pay money for it,' said Malachi, opening a full wallet upon the counter in the shadow of his body. 'The police don't approve of that, I'm told. So people who're connected with the police don't do it – do they?'

The calm, opaque eyes assessed the roll of notes with interest. 'One can never tell what the police will do next, Mr Rouault. They think of the most absurd things. All zeal, no doubt!'

Malachi waited, unperturbed, for it was clear that the jeweller did not seriously believe the police had had any hand in sending these dangerously direct people to him for information. In a moment or two the scrupulously levelled-out voice said practically: 'In the back room here I might have something in your line.'

They followed him into a narrow little workshop, smoky

and close from an oil-stove. The door closed softly behind them. Fredericks said: 'I always do what I can for people. Especially if they've been a bit unfortunate. You'll understand that quite harmless souls have their setbacks with the police sometimes. I don't believe in penalising them for it over and over again – do you, sir?'

'No. I might even, if I thought the case warranted it, be disposed to lend them a helping hand.' Malachi detached a fold of notes in an absent-minded manner, and fanned them out on the littered table among the minute tools and emery dust and rouged rags, pinning them down with a tiny netsuke figure which was lying upon a shelf above. 'I don't go near the police myself – the appeal to law is the last resort in certain cases, don't you agree?'

He turned away with deliberate slowness to look round the room, but he felt the moment when the money vanished.

'Oh, yes, Mr Rouault, I can see that a fellow who had made mistakes could look for a fair deal from you. With most people, it's once a bad lot, always a bad lot. Take this little thing I was going to show you, now—' With impressive gravity he placed the netsuke upright in Malachi's palm, where it sat leering at him obscenely, while its owner looked on with his slight, regretful smile. 'This poor unlucky fellow I'm thinking about – if he brought me in even so unlikely a little thing as that, the police would be wanting to know where he got it, and hinting at a bit of light-fingered work on the way to it. Or if it was a cigarette-case, say, they'd be talking of picking pockets on a rush-hour train. All because he once got mixed up in a bad misunderstanding with them – case of

44

mistaken identity it was – and couldn't prove he was somewhere else at the time. So I won't deny I've sometimes helped him out without making any record of the purchase, or letting his name get into it anywhere. I'm all for giving a man fair play.'

Malachi raised his eyes from the hideous little figure, and encountered the guileless stare without a flicker of an eyelash. 'An unfortunate like that wouldn't have anything to fear from me,' he said, half-smiling. 'I don't believe in hounding a man, myself.'

'Well, of course, there are some things you can't pass over – like murder. The world couldn't carry on if we went to that extreme of living and letting live, could it? But a mild little fellow like this friend of mine – he wouldn't hurt a fly, Mr Rouault, I give you my word for it.'

'I'd like to know your friend, Mr Fredericks. I might be able to do something for him. We might be able to do something for each other.' He put down the netsuke with scrupulous care, on the spot where the notes had lain.

'He's inclined to be a nervous type – my friend. Appearances have so often been against him, you see.'

'Nobody would be more likely to respect his inclinations than I should. I have a soothing presence.'

'You could inquire for him,' said Mr Fredericks benignly, 'at an address I'll give you in Islington. He has a room over a newsagent's there. Just go into the shop, and ask for Jody. They'll understand, if you say you're from Fred.' He fished from a drawer in the table an end of soiled notepaper, and from behind his ear a stub of pencil, and wrote delicately, slanting a shadowy smile upward into Malachi's face as he surrendered the folded slip. 'You'll win your way into his confidence, Mr Rouault, I'm sure – just as you have into mine. That's if his nerves aren't worse. You never know with nervous afflictions, do you?'

Margaret thought of a timid little pickpocket sitting shivering in his room over the shop, straining his ears for every approaching footfall, every trill of the telephone, every clash of the latch below, wondering when either the police or someone worse would come inquiring for him. It was all very clear, except the single issue of what Mr Fredericks expected them to be able to get out of him. No doubt he could use money, but dared he market what he knew? And suppose it was really no more than a dip into an unknown pocket on a crowded tube train, as the jeweller had hinted? Suppose he had nothing to sell? Either that, or Fredericks was absolutely sure that he would be afraid to admit to having it. Or, of course, there was the possibility that Fredericks cared nothing at all for his friend's safety, so long as he himself knew nothing and patently threatened nobody. Jody might well be held to be expendable. But she could not quite believe it. Even a shady business needs to maintain its reputation upon a certain level, and the price had been too modest, as the manner was too light-hearted, for a complete betrayal.

Malachi took the thought from her mind, as soon as they had put a hundred yards and a sharp street-corner between themselves and the dark little doorway of the pawnshop and were plunging arm-in-arm down the steps of the Underground.

'He's quite sure we shall draw a blank. It wasn't even

worth holding us off, he's so sure of it. Jody won't admit to knowing anything at all. Maybe, for a consideration, he'll go so far as to tell us what we know already, that he stole some bits of jewellery – somehow, somewhere – and knew nothing whatever about their having anything to do with a murder until today's papers. Or more likely until Fred sent him a message last night. He won't know the man he got them from, not even what he looks like. It will have been dark, he won't even have seen more than the back of his head. He won't know anything.'

'Still, you're going to try him, aren't you?'

'We've nothing else to try.'

'No!' said Jody MacClure, flattening his narrow shoulders against the flowered wallpaper suddenly, as though he were preparing to stand off an attack. 'I shouldn't know him again. I never got a good look at him, I tell you. He was one in a big crowd coming out of the Haymarket, and I took good care not to see him too well. What did Fred send you here for? He'd got no right. I can't tell you nothing. I never saw his face, how could I know him again?'

Margaret, who had taken no part in the long, low-toned arduous duologue, found herself marvelling afresh at Jody's air of extreme respectability. He was older than she had expected, probably in the sixties, and had the inexpensive neatness of a blameless clerk, with well-trimmed grey hair, unobtrusive hands and a deprecating little nervous cough. Nothing about him suggested an irregular way of making a living; only something in the deep grey folds of his worn face, and the alertness of the small brown eyes in their veined

47

hoods, gave him an appearance of being in disguise within this worthy exterior, if not in ambush. It was not at all a disagreeable face. She found herself believing what the jeweller had told them, that, whatever his habits with regard to property, Jody would not hurt a fly.

'I've told you, nothing you say here goes outside the room. Never mind what we're doing; I promise you you shan't be dragged into it. But you must have noticed *something* about him. You were near enough to get your hand into his pocket. What was it, his overcoat pocket? No, it was a warm night, he wouldn't be wearing a coat.'

'It was his left-hand jacket pocket. I was concentrating on what I was doing. I've told you all I know. It was on the night of September the third, outside the Haymarket, just as the crowd was coming out after the performance, and he come out with 'em, I'm telling you—'

'And you were hanging about outside. So you must have seen his face!'

'I never did! I worked my way across among the groups, and see him standing there with his shoulder turned to me, just where the stream coming out was going both ways round him, and him with both hands up lighting a cigarette—' He halted violently, perceiving his mistake.

'So the light of a match or a lighter was directly on his face! But you didn't see it!'

'His back was turned on me, and it was my chance, while his hands were occupied. I never looked at his face or anything. I just tried his pocket, and that was all I got. You don't have no call to pick me up like that, I've told you all I know.'

But he had not; that was plain in his vehemence, which at another time he might have been able to control. He had not only seen the elusive face plainly on the night of September the third, but last night after Fred's messenger had left him he had seen it again, seen it constantly, with perilous clarity, wishing all the time that he could erase it from his mind. The face of a murderer is not a good thing to know too well. Unless, of course, he is already in handcuffs, or at least paraded for identification in the safe custody of the police. Then knowledge might mean security instead of danger.

'I tell you again,' said Malachi patiently, 'we won't involve you in anything we do. But can't you see that it would pay you to help us? You want him found, you want him safely locked up, because you'll be safer then. Identify him for us, and somehow we'll manage the rest without dragging you in. Keep your mouth shut, and it looks as if he's going to get away with it. Heaven help you, then, if he finds out who you are, and how much you even *may* know. At least you must have sized him up, age, bulk, clothes. He must have looked a good touch, or you wouldn't have bothered to pick his pocket.'

'He was tall, and nearly as broad as you – and somewhere about your age, maybe. Yes, he was dressed all right, he looked smart enough.'

'Not in evening dress?'

'No, it was a dark lounge suit. That's all I know, so help me.'

He licked his meek, mauve lips, and flashed the quick little eyes from Malachi's face to Margaret's. It began to look as if that was all they were going to get out of him.

49

And yet he was tempted; Margaret could see it in the speculative yet timorous glance, that could not rest nor confront them directly, and yet could not leave the exploration of their faces for long. After all, how did he know they might not be effective, and really relieve him of this nightmare shadow upon his almost blameless little life? If he helped them, there might be heavenly security, and pay as well. They had money to spare; he had an earnest of it already.

'Yes,' she thought, intuition stirring vehemently, 'he wants to talk, if he dared. Only not the face! He isn't going to admit to anybody, ever, until the murderer's in custody, that he could recognise the face. So there must be something else. But if that was the full extent of their encounter, what else can there be?'

Gently, avoiding the suddenness which might surprise him into defence again, she said: 'What became of the other thing you took out of his pocket? We don't want it. But it might help if you let us see it. That's all – it might help.'

Malachi's sharp silence was the only violent thing that happened. Jody sat, quiet, looking at Margaret, and it seemed to her that his nervous tension had perceptibly relaxed, now that she had put her finger inescapably on his secret.

'There's nothing to lose,' she said, carefully indifferent. 'We're not asking you to come forward.'

He had it on him, of course. When he had made up his mind to trust them as far as he must, he plunged a trembling hand into his inside pocket, and took out a little wad of cotton-wool, from which he disentangled and shook out upon his palm a tiny, glittering thing.

* * *

Margaret drew in her breath sharply, and closed her fingers upon Malachi's arm. They sat staring in fascination at the minute sapphire petals, the wisps of green enamel leaf, the thin stem. The reality was more flower-like, more true in colour even than the painted copy. The problem of disposal of bulky jewellery in a well-fitting suit must have caused the murderer to leave only small, flat pieces in the pockets of his jacket. This tiny, elegant thing could not have disturbed the set of his clothes by so much as a visible ripple.

'This was all?' said Malachi, in a low voice.

'Yes, this and the brooch. If there was another o' these, I missed it.'

'You didn't try disposing of this?'

Jody grinned, though a sweat of anxiety stood on his lip. 'What d'you take me for? Too identifiable by half, that is. I reckoned it would have to be slipped abroad, or wait a long time till the shindy died down. Another thing – I knew nothing about a murder, but I figured these were stolen before I lifted 'em. Who goes round carrying pebbles in his jacket pocket? It was the cigarette-case I tried for, only I picked the wrong side. And now, after this business . . .'

'It's still identifiable – only more dangerous than ever!'

The bright, small eyes shrank, smiling. 'More valuable, too – to somebody!' Even his smile was agonised, yet its anxiety was sweetened by the compensating thought of the lucrative hold he had over another human being. Yes, he knew enough to find the man who had carried that minute and revealing treasure, if only he dared exercise his advantage.

'It might be worth a fair sum to me,' said Malachi, holding down his tone with difficulty from too much eagerness.

'Not as much as it will be to somebody else,' said Jody softly.

'But my price wouldn't have a funeral attached to it.'

'I can take care of myself, thank you!' But his eyes blinked rapidly, and he wiped the sweat from his lip nervously.

'You could be too ambitious. Wouldn't you rather take a sensible hundred for it, and stay alive? And free? Thousands won't be any use to you if you make just one slip handling a man like that.'

Jody had thought of that, too, he was thinking of it all the time.

'And, don't forget, this thing happens to be mine. I could call a policeman now, if I liked, and turn you in for being in possession of it. Instead, I'm offering you a hundred for it, and no trouble.'

The narrow, womanish hand closed jealously upon the ear-clip at Malachi's slight movement towards it. 'You could raise that offer a lot before I'd be interested. In fact, mister, I doubt if you can afford this little lot – I doubt it very much! Sold in the right market, it's worth more than you could raise.'

'It might be,' said Malachi, 'if you were immortal. But somehow I don't think you'd live to collect from the customer you're thinking of.'

'You can let me alone to take care of that.' But the very asperity of his voice was a reaction from the agony of dread that chilled the ardour of his greed. He could not make up his mind to part easily with his advantage,

THE ASSIZE OF THE DYING

and yet he doubted himself if he could ever screw up his courage to use it. Horribly torn, he trembled and writhed, trying to make up his mind.

'You can save your breath, you're not getting it. I'm not parting. You wouldn't call the police – you promised this was between you and me, and you won't go back on it, I know your sort. Well, I'm keeping this, see? I'll have plenty of time to plan out how to use it.'

Malachi and Margaret exchanged a quick glance. It was plain that they could not persuade him to give up his perilous asset, and the terms of their approach to him precluded any measures of compulsion.

'All right, then, keep it. But at least let me have a closer look at it. Give it to Miss Manton, if you don't trust me – you know she'll hand it back to you.'

On these terms Jody surrendered it pliantly enough, himself laying it upon Margaret's outstretched palm.

'Open the clip, Margaret – hold it with your handkerchief. I expect the prints, if there ever were any, are gone to blazes long ago, but no need to deface any marks that may be left. And you, my lad, if you want to keep your asset at its most valuable, don't handle it with your fingers.'

Through the lawn, Margaret's finger-tips delicately parted the little blue flower from its flat, silver lobe, patterned inside and out with a fan of fine indentations. Malachi leaned his cheek against hers, and they studied it together, closely, breathlessly. Then Margaret's hand shook, the clip sprang to again and the blue speedwell fell and glittered upon the reed mat.

On the silver inner surface they had seen the remnant

of a small brown stain; the smooth planes had been rubbed clean by much handling, but a dull, dry line of brown, fine as a hair, still coloured every indentation for a length of half an inch, the last lingering traces of Zoë Trevor's blood.

She could not look at her fingers, that evening, without seeing again the thin corrosion of brown in those grooves; and her depression, her sense of having been very near to the truth and yet somehow having missed it, weighed on her like a gathering storm. She drifted through her solitary tea, and smoked the one cigarette she allowed herself before beginning preparations for the evening. Tomorrow was dedicated to a friend who seldom came to town, and for one day at least her fever would have to cool itself as best it could. But even if she could have rejoined Malachi early tomorrow, where were they to go next? They had already talked it over and over between them, and arrived nowhere. the ear-clip stayed with Jody MacClure, safe but unfruitful, and even if they could induce him to part with it, what use were they to make of it? It was valuable only when he chose to provide them with the face that went with it. Or, of course, from his point of view, when he took action to contact the man from whom he had stolen it.

As anonymous as ever, the murderer moved freely, somewhere about the world, immune, no path leading to him; and, unless something caused him to break cover, for all Margaret could see he might go invisible for ever. Now if they could keep a watch upon the activities of Jody MacClure, and he should attempt the contact he feared and desired so much, on which his greed and his terror alike were centred—

54

'But he won't!' said Margaret aloud, with absolute conviction. 'He'll sweat blood planning it, he'll always be meaning to make the approach, but he'll never manage to do it. When it comes to the point his nerve will fail him. He won't be able to bring himself to use the thing, or to let go of it.'

And what, after all, was he to do? She began to wonder about that. How could the approach be made, supposing he knew only his man's face, not his name and whereabouts? What did one do in a case like that? One could hardly put a notice in the 'Personal' Column—

Then she thought, why not? People read it. Almost everyone reads it - not every day, perhaps, but occasionally. And it isn't so difficult to say, 'I've got something it would pay you to be reasonable about,' in terms which will pass by every eye but the ones for which it is intended. If Jody MacClure hasn't the nerve to do it, why shouldn't someone else draw the wood for him? How is the murderer to know who drew up the advertisement? All he'll be sure of is that whoever drew it up knows something, knows far too much.

Put yourself in the murderer's place, she told herself, growing excited. At this moment he's already alerted, because this morning's papers carried the item about the brooch being found and identified. He'll be watching the papers more closely than usual. Now *he* knows that he lost two bits of jewellery from his pocket that night, not just one, and the odds are a thousand to one on, that where the one went, the other went too. Ergo, he knows that whoever let Fredericks have the brooch to sell for him has retained the ear-clip, and is well aware now of its significance. He'll have spent quite a lot of time recalling everything recallable about that ear-clip, and he, of all people on earth, knows only too well that the lobe of Zoë's ear bled a little. He may not *know* that the clip is marked. He'll certainly fear that it may be. Supposing, then, that he suddenly comes up against a 'Personal' which is unmistakably inviting him to a date with some unknown person, to talk business about that clip. Will he go? I don't think he can afford not to go. With the money to pay – or the means to make payment unnecessary. Because only one person, he'll be sure, could have issued the invitation, and that's the one person in the world who knows too much, and must be prevented from passing on what he knows – the man who picked his pocket that night. Yes, he'd be very interested indeed in an appointment like that. It wouldn't matter much whether the advertiser brought the clip to the meeting with him or not – once he was quiet for good it wouldn't be important, because no one would know where it was lifted from, or be able to identify the man who had it in his pocket on the night of the murder.

She had reasoned herself into a kind of hypnosis. But it was already too late for this evening's papers. No, perhaps not too late for the last *Gazette*, if Charlie was at the office. Better an evening sheet than a daily. There was too much variety by daylight, but everyone reads the last editions at night, with really only two papers to choose from, or at most three.

She ground out her half-smoked cigarette, and sat down with pencil and paper to compose her bait. Several times she crossed out her efforts impatiently, but at last it read to her like the right blend of candour and mystery.

56

* * *

'SPEEDWELL: Early meeting to our mutual advantage. Name time and place. LIGHT FINGERS.'

It was a cocky junior who answered her ring at the office, and he told her that Mr Manton was out on an important assignment, and might be out of town overnight. However, it seemed that as a special favour to Miss Manton the front office would accept her 'Personal' by telephone, so that it could be included in tonight's final edition – though such a late insertion was, the junior intimated, most irregular. She dictated it slowly and distinctly. Spoken, it sounded curiously commonplace, and she suffered a revulsion of feeling, and half wished it back again. Nothing could possibly come of it! But there was no withdrawing now; and even if the bait caught nothing, there was at least nothing to lose by the attempt.

She bathed and dressed, and wound her way down the three flights of stairs in the narrow old house, three times encountering her reflection upon the dim landings cold in the late autumn evening. A fair girl, very slender in a dark dress, with a pointed chin and a plaintive width of brow, searching her own face at every turn of the staircase. She seemed to herself not quite real, as though she had dispatched the vital part of herself somewhere else upon a necessary errand, and could not get it back in time to be convincing in the eyes of her uncle and her uncle's guest. She was waiting all the time for the evening papers to thrust their way through the letter-box and drop with a heavy sibilance upon the hall floor; and she was thinking of the quick magnificence of Zoë Trevor, and its unbelievable extinction. No one had ever been more alive than she, nor left a greater devastation round her when she died; not even the Spanish countess.

It was only two days since she had seen Sir Robert Wyvern in court, yet when he came into the full light of the drawing-room she was astonished at the change in him. The monumental brow had lost its marble smoothness; faint, unaccustomed furrows of perplexity marked it painfully. The heavily correct face, long and immobile, between aristocratic and equine, had sagged from its perfect tension, and for the first time he looked middle-aged, almost old. She thought at first, instinctively: 'He's ill!'

But in a moment she knew that he was afraid. Not rebelliously, not combatively afraid, but deep in a regretful resignation. 'Good God!' she said to herself, 'he believes in this curse!' And the mere fact of his quiescence under that belief seemed to bring death into the house with him. She looked round the bright room, silver, cream and rose, as lofty as its own breadth, and it seemed to her to have dulled with his coming.

Mr Justice Manton came down as they were drinking sherry, and his granite presence, unshaken by the preoccupations and doubts of lesser men, seemed to thrust his colleague, by contrast, a step nearer to disintegration.

'Charlie not home yet? Has he telephoned?'

'I rang up his office, and it seems he's on a job that may take him out of town for tonight. Sherry, Uncle John?'

'Thank you, Margaret! They didn't say what chimera he's chasing now? It seems an unreal existence to me,' admitted the Judge, taking his guest by the arm and drawing him to the fire.

'It has change and variety,' said Sir Robert. 'These boys came out of the Forces at the wrong time and the wrong age, it seems to me. They were overtuned before they were even grown up, they can't get back to a normal pitch now. All they can do is try to accelerate every job to their own speed, and as one collapses move on to another, and speed that up until they wreck it. It takes a lot of one-act melodramas like that to make up a lifetime. I often think it must seem an endlessly dreary business to them.'

'The trouble is that they have every gift except application,' said the Judge roundly. 'Charlie's certainly run through several – one-act melodramas, as you say – since he came out.'

'Application!' Sir Robert smiled wryly into the fire over his glass. 'That's a virtue for which there was neither time nor need in their world of enforced celebrity. I suppose as their physical apparatus slows down the tempo will become a little easier. It seems hard to have to wait for old age to get a little peace.' He looked up at Margaret. 'The papers haven't come in yet?'

'Not yet!' She had started at the apposite question. Sherry spilled on to the skirt of her dress.

'You haven't been in court today?' asked the Judge.

'No – no, I was wondering if there would be any more developments in this wretched Trevor business. The brooch, you know. It seemed curiously vindictive of fate to turn the thing up the day after Stevenson died.'

'I don't see that it alters the case. You're not letting Stevenson's little vengeance prey on your mind, Robert, are you? You conducted a perfectly fair and balanced case, and obtained a completely justified conviction. The truth is, you've been overworking grossly for months; you must expect to feel the effects of it sooner or later. You haven't actually any qualms about your safety, have you?'

'I have qualms about the verdict,' said Sir Robert in a low voice.

'I have none. Our business is justice, and we have done justice. A medieval story, however dramatically apposite, alters nothing.'

'I wonder, 'said Sir Robert sadly, 'if our conception of justice is not sometimes a little arrogant.'

Over dinner in Mr Justice Manton's house they forswore all such topics of conversation. The old man drew on his amazingly catholic relaxations for his table-talk, and brought out in his lighter moments a kind of marmoreal charm, gracious but cold, which shed light about him without warmth. Not until they were sitting over the fire in the drawing-room once again, and the papers rattling through the letter-slot made Margaret spring up from her coffee, did they return to the case of Louis Stevenson.

'I doubt if there's anything to worry you tonight, Robert. The whole sensation will drain away slowly, as they always do, without giving us the satisfaction of seeing it end. Doubts about the facts of guilt and death,' he said, with surprising gentleness, 'are occupational risks in our profession. They show that the heart is still alive to one's fallibility – that one is, in fact, still fit to practise.'

Margaret had closed the door after her in order to give

herself time to open the paper in the hall, and search the 'Personal' column for her advertisement. It was there, with the usual half-dozen others. It looked so unobtrusive that she wondered if anyone would really be jolted into attention by it, and bother to answer. Sir Robert might well be a fair test case, for he would certainly open at once to this page, since it was here that the few bare paragraphs on the Stevenson case were deployed for the evening, under unjustified headlines: 'Assize of the Dying: Latest Developments.' What the item actually stated was that there were no developments since the identification of the broch, already reported in the dailies. Mr Fredericks' name and address had been kept out of print; but for the accident of his inheritance they would certainly never have been confided to Malachi.

Beneath the smaller type of the column, the capitals she had insisted on for 'SPEEDWELL' stood out well. She felt a little encouraged. Readers to whom the name meant nothing might easily slide past it and never recognise what they had read, but a man whose mind was on that ear-clip should not, surely, miss its significance. She refolded the paper carefully, and took it in and gave it to Sir Robert.

He opened it, as she had expected, to the page from which his accepted curse confronted him, and read impassively. His only comment was a quiet sigh.

'Nothing new? I'm not surprised. It will pass, *diminuendo*, as these things do.'

There was a sudden sharply indrawn breath, like the acknowledgement of a stab of pain. Sir Robert was sitting erect, the paper spread in his hands, his gaze frozen and still.

'What is it? What's the matter?'

'Oh – nothing new! This – oh, no, it's no more than a queer coincidence, just a word that cropped up out of context. Do you ever catch an echo from years ago, like a bell ringing?' He read out slowly, incredulously, Margaret's advertisement. 'Speedwell! It's years since I saw the word printed, even – probably not since the programmes. Do you remember?'

'I remember.'

He read and re-read the single line, his broad brow gradually drawn down into a shadowy and painful frown. Margaret could see his lips stirring strangely upon the words, and she received from him, as it were through the charged air, a sensation of almost unbearable agitation and sadness. When he finally put the paper aside and looked up at them, his eyes were hollow and dark, staring at something far beyond and apart from the cream-and-rose walls of the Clevely Square drawing-room. She felt as if she had approached a mirror, and encountered face to face a reflection which was not her own. He had seen and noticed her message, if a test was what she had wanted; but what was it he had seen? Nothing she had written into it, but some fantastic recollection of his own, something from the remote past.

Afterwards, when he had left them, she asked her uncle: 'Why was he so disturbed by that notice? What did the word "speedwell" mean to him, to upset him so much?'

Mr Justice Manton looked at her for a long moment in silence, and when he spoke his voice was deceivingly calm and untroubled.

'Robert's in a low state just now, and has this case very much on his conscience. I'm afraid everything that can

THE ASSIZE OF THE DYING

conceivably be linked up with Zoë Trevor leaps automatically to his eye – whether it has anything to do with
her or not. He knew her very well at one time. It was
before your day, of course, and the show's never been
revived, so the title's dropped out of remembrance these
days. *Speedwell* was the musical comedy in which she
made her first London success. She was seventeen then,
and Robert was – old enough to know better, but he
didn't.'

'He was in love with her, too?' said Margaret.

'He was engaged to her, for a short time. She had good
sense, and was fond of him in her way, and she broke it
off. He took it very hard. It's no wonder, really, that the
word hit him hard tonight.'

. He flashed a glance at her face, and stopped abruptly
there. Old men reminisce too much, but why involve the
young unnecessarily? He thought: 'We're all becoming
obsessed by this affair. Even Margaret is infected.' And
he was firmly silent, with that quality of silence which
she knew better than to disturb. What was the use of
elaborating? Robert had had some small articles of jewellery made for his darling, in the form of germander
speedwells, to commemorate her success. What were
they – dress-clips? – ear-rings?   He had forgotten
details. There remained only a recollection of loss, not to
be shared with the young. The young would be recalling
their own losses only too soon.

In the morning, before she left the house to meet her
friend, Margaret rang up Malachi's hotel, but he was
already out, and had left a message for her to the effect
that he had gone to the house in Hampstead with the

solicitor who was handling Zoë's estate, and expected to be involved in legal matters most of the day. She felt a distinct stab of disappointment which had nothing to do with the necessity for carrying the weight of her secret all day alone, but was somehow more intimately tangled with the sound of Malachi's voice in her ear, and the dark, level look of his disturbing eyes. To spend a whole day away from him was now curiously damaging to her equilibrium, as though she moved in a continual slight danger of vertigo. The day, however, passed. London and shopping and her friend's conversation revolved brightly round her, until she saw Maeve off at King's Cross, and took a taxi back to Clevely Square.

Charlie was in the bathroom, singing lustily. She banged on the door and adjured him not to be long, for it was already after six o'clock.

'Fine time to come home!' shouted Charlie, breaking off in the middle of '*La Donna è Mobile*'.

'You should talk, staying out all night! When did you get in?'

'Came home for lunch. I went straight to the office when I got into town this morning.'

'You're going to be out again tonight?' She had recognised all the signs of one of his total exits, when a trail of strewn garments, wet towels and slammed doors marked his passage through the house, and almost before she could greet him he had kissed her lightly and gone again. 'You don't live in this house,' she cried, thumping her palm against the door, 'you only haunt it.'

'You go and fetch your things, I'm coming out in a tick.' And by the time she was back from her bedroom he was just emerging, flushed and tousled, and plunging head-down for his own room to dress. In mid-flight, when it seemed they would pass with only a wild exchange of smiles, he caught her for an instant in the crook of his arm.

'Everything all right, Meg?' He smiled at her, his thin, long cheeks dimpling tenderly.

'Of course, idiot! Why not?'

He swung her on into the bathroom, and fled. All she saw of him afterwards was a wave of the hand from the front doorway, and a valedictory smile, as she came down the stairs dressed and refreshed, to look for the evening paper. It was early to expect an answer, her own notice had appeared only in the late editions, but she trembled with mingled eagerness and reluctance as she picked up the crumpled early *Gazette* which Charlie had just thrown down. The door, slamming loudly upon his spruce departure, made her start as at a pistol-shot. She drew breath deeply, steadying her heart against too much anticipation.

But it was there, first in the brief column, leaping to her eye instantly when she folded back the page:

'LIGHT FINGERS: St Lucian Martyr, south porch, eleven tonight. SPEEDWELL.'

As soon as she read it she knew that she had never really believed in it. She had speculated and dreaded, foreseeing all the strange meeting-places the unknown might have appointed her, but even the fear had been an imaginative fantasy; for now that she read the message and knew it for a reality, the fear was gone. She found herself chilled but calm, her mind moving upon practical necessities with a methodical deliberation. Eleven o'clock – a churchyard somewhere not very far from the Albert Hall. She would have to look it up on the map to be quite sure of its position, but she thought she remembered it. A rather large churchyard, with graves, and a lot of trees, its railings down since the war, its tower roofless and hollow, another of London's ghosts; and on either side of it, close but quiet, the discreet and deserted back streets of Kensington, more silent than forests, lonelier than country lanes.

She had thought at first, what a curious place to choose, and wondered if he might not be a little mad, to want to have his rendezvous surrounded so closely by blameless people and law-abiding homes; but now some curious characteristic of the whole invitation, the combined threat and bravado of the suggested hour, the unexpectedness of the place, with its cover of audacity and its many potential exits, filled her with a fear no longer imaginative and enjoyable, but sane, calculating and shrewd. He knew what he was about, this man; it was up to her to match him, and if she could, to think before him.

With the paper still clutched in her hand she lifted the telephone receiver, propped it between hunched shoulder and cheek, and dialled the number of Malachi's hotel. This time he was in. He sounded tired and a little on edge.

'Oh, hullo, it's you!' the strained voice warmed. 'Have a nice day? You're at home now?'

'Malachi,' she said directly, 'I want you to come out with me tonight. Come and call for me after dinner – about nine, and I'll explain all about it. Please, it's important, I've got something to tell you—'

He cut in so brusquely that she broke off in astonishment, letting his voice bear down hers: 'I can't! Not tonight! It isn't possible tonight, Margaret. Look, do something for me! Tomorrow morning let me come and see you, but tonight stay in and forget all about this damned business, for God's sake!'

'But, Malachi—'

She was about to tell him that tomorrow would be too late, that she needed him tonight, that the whole case might break tonight. She was about to say all the things she had instinctively wished to keep for his private ear and his presence, with which the telephone was no longer quite to be trusted. But she never began the recital. The step on the stairs was light as a young man's; when she heard it, and swung round wildly with the paper in one hand and the receiver in the other, Mr Justice Manton was half-way down the stairs, and watching her steadily as he came.

Exactly why she should, without any question, have taken it for granted that nothing could be confided to her guardian's ears, she never really knew. It was not that she did not like him, not even that if she had taken him into her confidence he would have found a way of preventing her from acting in the matter. It was purely instinctive. She simply was not on terms of confidence with him; it would have been like trying to translate herself into a different culture, and her story into an unfamiliar language. She covered herself at once, sounding casual and cool: 'Well, I rather specially wanted to see you. Couldn't you manage it? It really is quite important.' But her voice kept so jealous a composure that he could hardly be expected to believe in the urgency of her preoccupations, even if he had not been wrestling hard with his own.

'I've told you, I can't – not tonight. Have a night off, Margaret – go to bed early, don't think about sensations, don't even dream about them. I wish to God I'd never started you on this thing at all.'

'You didn't, it was my own doing. But listen, I—'

He had hung up. For a moment she could not believe it, she hung on the line waiting for him to speak again and he did not. She replaced the receiver slowly, and raised to her uncle a mechanical and arduous smile. She was walking away into the drawing-room when he said mildly: 'If that's the *Gazette*, Margaret—'

'Oh yes,' she said, a little confused, and handed it over without unfolding it from the tight, small folds into which she had pressed it. 'I've finished with it.' She had certainly read the only item of any interest to her. When she had escaped into the drawing-room from the old man's sight, she flew to the mirror to see how much her face might have betrayed. That look of shock and anger, as though a door had been slammed on her, startled even herself. The Judge was a subtle observer, with a trained eye for agitation and nervous tension, even the kind that kept itself well in control, with admirable colour and calm. She composed herself fiercely, moderated the wide stare, relaxed the lines of her face with troubled, flexing fingers. The south porch of St Lucian Martyr, eleven tonight—

Mr Justice Manton, finding the 'Personal' column folded outward, read down it quietly, and found what he

was seeking. Margaret at the telephone, incandescent
with still excitement, had provided more than enough
light for him to read by. Robert's instinct had certainly
been sound. The speedwell was one of Zoë Trevor's trinkets, the deal to be completed 'to our mutual advantage'
was a deal in silence; and who had need of silence about
Zoë stolen jewellery, except the man who had killed her?
He did not know who Malachi was, Malachi whom she
had wanted to go with her tonight, and who had declined
so abruptly. But then, there were so many things he did
not know. He no longer knew, it seemed, who had murdered Zoë Trevor. It was the first time in his adult life
that he had ever consented to relinquish a conviction
upon such inward evidence, but it had happened; his
superb certainty was gone, and the beginning of disintegration was already vibrating in him where the main-
spring of his being had lain.

He was pleased with Margaret. If she had to keep so
dangerous an appointment, at least she was going about
it wisely. She had come well before the hour, approaching quietly from the darkest side of the churchyard,
where the trees leaned against the high rear wall of a
block of houses, and only a passageway and flight of
steps came up between the buildings from the lower level
of the next street. She had made a circuit of the church,
keeping always within the shadows of the untrimmed
trees and stepping softly through the long, tangled grass;
and then she had taken her station in a thicket of bushes
close to the low wall on the south-east side, from which
the sawn-off inch-long ends of railings protruded sadly.
From there she could see into the south porch, and she

had two ways of escape open to her, over the single foot of wall into the broad, deserted cul-de-sac behind the tall houses, where a few garageless cars stood draped and ghostly, or back down the steps by the way she had come. She could hardly have found a better place, unless, of course, she had joined Mr Justice Manton inside the broken shell of the church itself.

He had gone there before her, so that she might have no reason to suppose that she was followed; and no doubt she had accepted with relief his early retirement to his room, and believed him to be there still. He spared a thin smile for the irony of an uncle telling so old a lie to evade the watchfulness of his niece, and getting away with it! He had climbed over a broken section of wall to enter the deserted church, and then taken care to provide a quicker and easier exit by unlocking, with considerable labour and noise, the vestry door, which had been left with the key in the lock within. The door swung well, considering its neglected state, with very little sound.

Now that the hour was drawing near, and from the empty windows he had seen Margaret dissolve herself into the darkness of the trees and grow purposefully still, he began to rehearse his exit. Only when someone approached the porch would he leave the shelter of the walls and take to the trees. He must see the man's face, and that was all he needed.

He had come as much for that as to look after Margaret. If she had been the only consideration, he could as easily, and far more safely, have confronted her with what he knew and what he guessed, and kept her from the meeting by force, if necessary. Instead, he was here. He had come for the man. Since the bait was so plainly Margaret's, there would presumably be only one man; and he would be the murderer.

Strange that so intact and intense a quietness could live in London. The churchyard, perhaps three-quarters of an acre of it, made its own forest, old trees above, long grass and leaning stones below, utterly unlit: an olive-green darkness, deeply opaque, within the clearer dark of the night. On three sides, but distant, the curtained and shuttered faces of large, quiet houses, their gates giving upon the broad cul-de-sac and two narrower through streets, little used by any traffic except the cars of the residents and, by day, the delivery vans of those who served them. On the fourth side, the high wall and the blank backs of those other houses between which the hollowed stone steps slid away to the passage and the mews below, furtive and shadowy. Nowhere here was there much light. One lamp at the end of the cul-de-sac, another at the most distant corner of the churchyard, where the two streets crossed. Occasionally, somewhere within call, a footstep, once even the steps of two people, and the attenuated threads of their voices. Then silence and loneliness again.

He continued to watch the formless darkness in which Margaret stood concealed, and presently in the silence he was aware of a movement which certainly did not emanate from Margaret. It was infinitely soft and slow, a faint rustling in the grass, the snap of a twig as it scraped across a sleeve. Margaret's bushes stirred once as she parted the branches to see more clearly.

Everything seemed to become more warily still. Then, shadowy among the trees, the Judge saw a man's figure grow out of the obscurity, moving step by step towards the church. He had come from the direction of Kensington High Street, and stepped over the wall into the grass to approach without sound. He was tall and young, and the brim of a soft hat was drawn low over his face, so that he had no identity. The Judge's eyes were accustomed to the darkness by now, but even in the build and movements of this figure he found nothing to recognise or note.

Margaret had a nearer and clearer view of that large young form. She made an unwary movement, and the bushes quaked once, no more than a shudder, but the quick ear caught it. He sprang round on her, and for an instant was absolutely still, sensing rather than seeing her. She cried suddenly, in a gasp of frantic disbelief: 'Malachi' and then, breaking from her hiding-place, ran to the low wall, and flung herself over it into the wide, blind street, and ran wildly along the pavement towards the distant lamp.

'Margaret!'

He crashed after her, surging through the bushes, leaping the wall and swearing aloud at the unexpected drop below. The curious, uneven double rhythm of their steps, the sharp staccato of her heels, the heavier beat of his rubber-soled shoes, re-echoed between the tall houses, diminishing slowly. The quietness came back almost before Mr Justice Manton had dragged open the vestry door and threaded the jungle of sharp-set bushes to stare after them.

Margaret reached the corner of the street, and for a moment hesitated in a stupor of bewilderment, having no reason to go one way rather than another. She heard him bounding after her, heard him call: 'Margaret!' with an urgency which drove her forward like a blow. She was not running anywhere in particular, she was merely running away from belief, away from realisation. Instead of going towards the remote and lulling continuo of the traffic in the High Street, she turned aside and plunged into the side-street, where the light was as subdued and the vague shadowy spaces between fence and fence as unpeopled as in the corner by the churchyard.

Twice, realising that she was about to meet a late stroller, she checked to a rapid walk and heard Malachi's feet slowing after her. She felt very tired, but as soon as the innocents were gone she began to run again. And yet she had not tried to speak to anyone she met. She was not thinking at all, every instinct and every energy she had left were concentrated on running away.

Malachi was gaining rapidly. She could hear his long, angry breaths and feel his nearness; and in a passage off Greville Street he caught her at last. His arm took her hard about the body, and pulled her round to face him, his left hand caught her right wrist as she threw up her arm. He thought she had meant to strike him, or ward him off, but actually she was going to do no more than steady herself by clutching at his shoulder. He held her hard against him, for fear she should break loose again. They were both panting, and their eyes, staring despairingly, met in mutual indignation. She had not realised until then that she felt no fear of him, and had not been running to preserve her life, but rather her dignity. It was all, in the end, a little ridiculous.

'Oh, no, you don't! What's the idea, running off like that? What are you doing here at all? I told you to stay at

73

home, didn't I? How did you follow me? How did you find out anything about it?'

'Let me go!' But after one tentative contortion she did not struggle, for he was much too strong for her. 'Leave me alone! I don't want to talk to you.'

'But you're going to. You're going to tell me what you were doing there, and why you had to run off like a scalded cat as soon as I saw you.'

'I'm not going to tell you anything. Why should I? I'm not accountable to you for what I do. Malachi, you're hurting me!'

'I'm sorry!' he said instantly but sulkily, and somewhat relaxed his grip, though warily. 'But I've got to understand— My God, it's all crazy! I thought you were safe at home, and I needn't worry about you. I suppose *you* saw that damned "agony" in the *Gazette* too, and guessed what it was all about? Or was it *you* who put it in?' The thought was new to him, his voice grew loud with fury, realising at once how easily this was possible. He shook her by the wrist. '*Was* it you?'

'Yes, it was!' she said, suddenly hopelessly calm. 'I rang you up this morning, intending to tell you about it, but you'd gone out already. And then this evening you wouldn't listen to me.'

'You never tried to tell me it was anything like that!' he protested, raging. 'As though I'd have let you do such a damned silly thing—'

'I couldn't go into details, my uncle came down, I had to pass it off pretty casually. And you rang off, you never gave me a chance. But it didn't matter,' she said bitterly, 'you'd seen it yourself, it seems, and knew what it meant without being told.'

74

'Well, how could I miss it, knowing what I knew? I thought it was Jody MacClure, trying to make one big touch and get out while he was safe. What else could I think? And you came down here alone to see what happened! My God!' he groaned, 'what I could do to you for taking a chance like that, you crazy fool!'

They had begun to walk on again, her arm dragged tightly through his, his hand still gripping her wrist. They stared ahead into the dark and the pools of lamplight, with angry, embittered eyes.

'And that doesn't explain why you took one look at me, and ran for your life.'

She was silent, hating him; but his own phrase had stabbed him into understanding. His step wavered for a moment. He went on, in a voice faint with fury: 'You don't mean to say you thought that *I*— You thought *I'd* put that answer in the *Gazette* tonight? When I appeared, you thought I was keeping that date with Jody because *I'd made it*?'

Her continued silence answered him sufficiently clearly.

'Thank you! It's nice to know that after all this, you think I'm Zoë's murderer. *Cui bono*, and all that! Don't be such an idiot! If I was the one who had cause to shut Jody's mouth, don't you think I could have done it yesterday?'

'While I was there with you?' she said, angry in her turn.

'I could have gone back without you, couldn't I? Why on earth should I risk answering an advertisement like that, just to get a quiet meeting with him, when I knew perfectly well where to find him alone whenever I chose?'

'It might have been safer to get him away from his room,' said Margaret, hotly arguing a case in which she did not believe, in which she had never believed for more than one disastrous moment.

'And in any case, if *I* were the man, why on earth should I take the trouble ever to meet him again? Why should I ever have considered paying him *or* killing him? He had long enough to take a good look at me yesterday, didn't he? Did he show any sign of recognising me for the man? And do you think he was the kind to keep a straight face and brazen it out if he *had* known me again? So what had I got to fear from him?'

'Then what *were* you doing there?' she asked more gently.

'Exactly what you were doing, I suppose. I saw the answer in the paper tonight. I was waiting to see who came to keep the appointment, of course. That's why I was early on the spot, I wanted a good place to lie up and watch from.'

Margaret admitted, her step slackening: 'You *were* early. That's why you startled me so much. I wasn't prepared for you.'

'Well, did you think I'd turn down meeting you for some ordinary thing?' he asked, still smarting. 'I thought you were safe at home, out of range. That's the way I wanted you. I thought with luck I might be able to tell you, tomorrow, who it was. I didn't have to tell you, you decided for yourself that it was me!'

Margaret lowered her head and walked beside him in

bitter silence, the swing of her light hair hiding her face even when they passed under a lamp. In a moment he began to be uneasy and, having tried in vain to catch a glimpse of the expression she was so assiduously hiding, he halted abruptly and drew her face to face with him again. Obstinate still, she would not look up, but pressed her forehead into his shoulder.

'Margaret, what's the matter? Margaret, look at me!'

She was crying with fury and shame, but very softly.

'Oh, lord! Margaret, don't – please!' He began to melt into alarm and dismay, stroking her hair. 'Oh, Margaret, darling! If you cry, you'll have me saying I *did* do it, anything you like, anything to please you.'

She lifted her face to him, stained, ill-tempered, vaguely lovely in the half-light where they stood. Malachi kissed her. They were both trembling.

'I never really thought you'd done it,' said Margaret in a grudging whisper. 'Only for a moment, anyhow. You startled me, and when I made that movement and you heard me – well, I just lost my head and ran, without thinking at all. And all the time I knew it was only you, but by the time I'd started thinking I was already running, and I was ashamed to stop. I didn't want to face you, because I'd made it look as if I really believed you were a murderer – as if I were afraid of you.'

'And weren't you?' asked Malachi, with a last impulse of anger.

'Idiot, don't you suppose I should have made straight for a main street if I'd been afraid of you?'

Her subtlety confounded him, and her tears had brought him to heel so sharply that he no longer knew how to argue with her.

'You *wanted* me to catch you?'

'I did and I didn't,' she admitted bewilderingly, her lips against his cheek. 'But more particularly I did. I didn't know any other way to get out of the mess we were in.'

Malachi said helplessly into her hair: 'Margaret, darling, I do love you so. I couldn't bear you to run away from me.'

'I never shall again,' she said consolingly.

They clung together gently, there at the edge of the lamplight in the prim little street. A soft, fine rain had begun to fall, but they did not notice it.

'And we spoiled our one chance,' sighed Margaret at length, raising her head from his shoulder. 'After all the trouble I went to to make it! If anyone really did come to keep the appointment, we've missed him. He'll have gone long ago now – no point in going back.'

For some reason it no longer seemed so important to them; they could not keep their minds anchored to it.

'We'd better get under cover somewhere,' said Malachi, at last becoming aware of the rain. 'Let's go and find one of those all-night places and get something to eat, shall we? Somewhere where we can talk.'

But it seemed that they no longer needed to talk, for as they linked arms closely and stepped out together along the street they gazed at each other, from time to time, with dazzled and charmed eyes, and found nothing at all to say.

Mr Justice Manton, watching with consternation the flight of his niece, and the young man's angry pursuit of her, had some moments of fear and confusion which were so unfamiliar to his usual poise as to leave him, to some extent, a different man. He could not hope to overtake either of those active young people, even if he could have persuaded his dignified legs to break into a run; and it was for him an effort even to think of shouting after them. The logical deduction from the encounter was obviously that this Malachi must be the murderer, since he had certainly come to the appointment, and that Margaret, horrified by the discovery, was in flight from a danger which might well threaten her life.

Yet there was something quite remarkably improbable about the way they ran, not at all as the Judge would have expected a prospective victim to flee from a murderer. It was the young man who was making all the noise, actually calling after her as he ran: 'Margaret!' in tones peremptory and indignant, even amazed, more like a frantic lover than a villain at bay. So perhaps Mr Justice Manton's perturbation was calmed at the heart by doubts, even before Margaret reached the corner; after which point it died altogether.

In the stretch of lighted street rising gently ahead of the cross-roads where Margaret had checked, a man was walking firmly and decorously towards her, a small figure yet, but already aware of her. If she had run straight on she would have met him within a minute. Instead, she turned aside and bolted into the narrow, dark side-street, where in an instant she and her pursuer were lost to sight. The Judge smiled in the darkness; he did not understand how far their relationship had gone, but he saw that no serious fear was involved in it. He drew breath gratefully, relaxing.

The approaching man, walking evenly, passed by the side-street without curiosity, and came on. Only then did the Judge remember that it was still only eight minutes to eleven, and a man walking towards him might be walking towards an appointment.

He could not withdraw into the interior of the church now without the risk of being seen. He drew back instead into the thickest clump of bushes, where Margaret had stood, and froze into stillness there, waiting. The man might turn in at any gate in the cul-de-sac, and let himself into his own house. But he did not. He walked along the pavement without stealth as far as the empty gateway of the churchyard, turned in there and made his way straight to the south porch. On the stone bench within he sat down composedly, and the darkness took all of him except a pair of long, black-clad legs, and one hand, a paler patch in the deep shadow, laid open and firm and still upon his knee.

Upon that hand, soon the only discernible shape in the shades, the one signature of human presence in the almost superhuman stillness, the Judge fixed his eyes, and wondered if this could be the hand which had obliterated Zoë Trevor, destroyed Louis Stevenson and defaced beyond erasure his own honour. Once the man had seated himself, he did not move, not even with the nervous tension of waiting. He had passed through the olive-green gloom of the trees as a large shape in movement, his dark overcoat and hat dappled faintly with confusing threads of light through the tangle of branches, from the lamp at the blind end of the street. Something in the deliberate shape had troubled the Judge with tremors of recognition, while he had no clear glimpses of either gait or face to make identification possible. Now the hand alone, large, calm and somehow tragic, lay resignedly on the crossed knees. It did not look like a murderer's hand. No agitation troubled its sad serenity.

Mr Justice Manton, in the silence and chill of the night, felt the seconds running out towards a judgement in which he, too, was involved. Justice had been his life, implication in an injustice was already a kind of death. His certainty was gone. At what precise moment he had lost it, whether at his friend's hands or Margaret's, he could not discern; but he knew that it was irrecoverable.

He saw again the face of the tired and disorganised old scholar in the dock, already indefinite, beginning to disintegrate, the angry eyes keeping to the last their integrity of accusation and hate, even when they seemed no longer to have colour or form enough to contain so much feeling. The Judge, watching the big, quiet hand, thought, was it you that made so many of us murderers?

The wind stirred a little, and a faint sheen was beginning to distil from the gloss of the rain upon leaves and grass and stone, making the darkness by a shade less dark. Somewhere a clock struck eleven, with infinite slowness, as though reluctant to acknowledge the inescapable hour.

As if the very sound had brought him, prompt to his time, there was suddenly another figure standing at the top of the steps which climbed from the street below. Pressed close to the high wall, silent and still, the man seemed no more than a very faint shape made by irregularities in the stone. He had chosen the darkest approach, and his coming had been rubber-shod and silent, but the man in the porch knew that he was there. The vague blur of the hand had lifted; the patient fingers were in the act of lighting a cigarette. He, at any rate, did not object to being seen. It was no part of his intention to go undetected.

The newcomer moved towards him slowly, and branches crossed and complicated the Judge's view of him, so that he was little more than a sensation of movement. When he came to within a couple of yards of the porch he was clear of the trees, but he had his back turned upon the spot where the Judge stood and he could have been any man of medium build and active years, in a large, loose raincoat which, by its just discernible shape in the dark, might have been of some dark fawn shade, and a soft dark hat which made him headless against the black interior of the porch. In the stillness which continued for a full minute after the slow approach had ceased, the two men were looking fixedly at each other.

The hand which held the cigarette came back into view, the little glow made a spark of red-gold in the dark. The man behind it, hidden within the inner blackness, said clearly:

'Speedwell, I presume!'

The syllables were not enough to identify the voice; before the Judge could quite believe he had detected a familiar tone, it was gone. After all, he thought, did Margaret really launch all this? Or was the threat of the advertisement a real threat, and was Margaret only one among all those who read it correctly? For if so, one of these two is a murderer and the other an accessory and a blackmailer.

82

The standing man, his hands still plunged deeply into the pockets of his raincoat, said: 'Yes!' in the whisper which has no individuality, and scarcely any sex.

The cigarette was dropped on to the stone flags, and trodden out under a shoe-heel. The hand which had held it was thrust into a coat pocket, and in an instant a shaft of light sprang up full into the newcomer's face. Mr Justice Manton had a momentary impression of a vivid brightness, in which the twigs leaped to sight like living things, and, printed blackly against this outburst of light, the outline of a head and shoulders in flat, clean-edged black, a paper cut-out of a man.

The man in the porch uttered something which sounded like: 'My God, you!' in a groan of amazement. Then from an insane confusion of small and almost soundless impressions, all simultaneous, Mr Justice Manton gathered these: the long raincoat rustled as a hand passed rapidly into and out of its pocket; the man in the porch, on the heels of his own exclamation, sprang up, or at least began to do so; there was a brief flash, and a small sound, a kind of dull thump, and the torch dropped upon the flags, rolled and went out. After the light had vanished, taking with it all outlines, all presences, the Judge was quite blind for a moment, and could not even find his way out from among the branches.

His own heart was so thunderous in its beat that he confused with it the retreating steps, light and quick, that rushed away down the narrow passage in the wall. When he groped his way to the porch, everything was already very quiet there.

He struck a match, and in the little, wavering light he saw the broken torch lying in a crack of the flags, and the big man slumped in the corner of the stone seat. His hat had fallen off, his head lolled sideways; and when the Judge thrust his hand into the breast of the coat it encountered the heat and stickiness of blood, but no heartbeat. The large, mournful brow, marble-white after the darkness, shone in weary placidity above half-closed eyes.

Sir Robert Wyvern had conducted his last prosecution, and the second of the four accused was on his way to the Assize of the Dying.

Mr Justice Manton went down the hollowed stone steps at a feverish, light run, along the more deeply shadowed side of the mews beyond and into the narrow street. This also was hardly more than a passage between the rear of a block of houses and a high garden wall, but at the far end on the left there was a lamp bracketed to the wall, and by its light he saw a man's figure just turning to the right and disappearing. The soft brown hat and the fawn raincoat were all he had time to see; and though this was, in fact, the first time he could be said to have seen them at all, they already appeared familiar to him, and were identifiable at a glance.

He began to run once again, on his toes, in long, soft steps, like a hunting animal; and when he reached the corner the figure was still in sight, moving out now into the quiet square where a few cars stood and an occasional late taxi cruised. The man was too far away to hear or suspect the pursuing footsteps, too distant to have much detail about him; but he was unmistakably the man. In the raincoat pocket reposed the gun which had just killed Sir Robert Wyvern, the silenced gun which had made so tiny a punctuation mark in the churchyard quiet and so irreparable a hole in the sick heart. But the murderer was walking with a leisured composure, firmly and jauntily, as though he had been at a symphony concert at the Albert Hall, and was playing over the music again in his own mind on his blameless way home.

As for the body, it would not suffer from the rain, or from being left alone a little while. Mr Justice Manton had left his friend with regret, but he had other duties. Besides, by all accounts he was very soon going to rejoin him. This other, this one who walked ahead of him, was the companion he must not lose.

It was not at all difficult to keep him in sight without drawing near to him, for here an occasional stroller was passing, and late theatre-parties making their contented way home. Besides, the man was superbly sure of his solitude. He was in reality leaving the scene quickly and purposefully, but all with an air of security and calm which showed that he had no idea of there being any witness. The Judge thought by how happy a chance Margaret had been swept off the scene, and hoped she was in good hands.

He had leisure to think as he walked, his eyes always upon those variable glimpses of the figure ahead. What he did not know was how Margaret had obtained the information which had enabled her to bait this trap. What he did know was that the bait itself had been Zoë's jewels, those speedwells which Robert had once given to her to celebrate her successful entry into her own world; and with them, inseparable from them, some dangerous information involved in their little blue stones. Now that he considered again the girl's intent interest in the advertisement of last night, her questions about Robert's reaction to it, her obvious excitement over tonight's answer, and her appeal to this young man of hers to join her in keeping the appointment, all these slight accumulations of suspicion became practical certainty that the hand behind the rendezvous was hers. She had found a way of causing the murderer to break cover. The disasters she had launched in the act were not really hers; sooner or later someone would have released them, since justice must be vindicated.

No, it was not Margaret's fault that she had caught more in her trap than she had bargained for. The young man Malachi – Mr Justice Manton's thoughts engaged with him almost pleasurably now, as though in these later stresses he had fallen into place and was no longer incomprehensible – obviously he had shared enough of Margaret's knowledge to understand the purport of her advertisement, without being aware of its origin. Those two innocents had cancelled each other out. The train to which they had set light would never do them any great damage.

But Robert had also known enough to recognise the connection of that 'Personal' with the dead Zoë and the gift he had once given her. Whoever feared revelations about those stolen trinkets feared them because they would bring the murder home to him. It had not been so difficult for Robert to come to that conclusion, because he was already obsessed by the conviction of his own part in the miscarriage of justice and had come to the point of full acquiescence in the price he must pay for it. So he, too, with Zoë and Louis Stevenson heavy upon his heart and mind, had come to keep the appointment and see the face of the man to whom he owed his ruin.

What he had intended then the Judge did not inquire of himself or anyone. He had seen his friend come openly, and openly wait for the guest not he, but another, had invited. He thought that Robert had not come with the intention of dying, but he was fairly sure that he had come with the possibility in his mind and with a great indifference to the result. It was not only the guilt for Stevenson; there was also the emptiness where Zoë had been. Above all, he had come because he must *know*. That was something the Judge understood perfectly; for he also had come in quest of the same destroying knowledge. Truth was truth, and justice justice, if it killed them both, as they had been assured it would.

And the last person who had understood the advertisement was the murderer himself, the active shadow under the trees ahead, threading the quiet streets with such a resolute step. And he had come in the expectation that the threat was genuine, that there really was one person in the world who had information which brought him into danger. He had come assured that there could be only one such person; and he had come not to buy it, not to steal it, only and simply to wipe it out. He had killed almost immediately, as soon as the man waiting for him in the porch identified himself with that word 'speedwell'. He had come to kill. Silence is expensive to buy. Killing is cheaper and more permanent.

He began to hurry, because his quarry was almost out upon the Cromwell Road and he could not risk losing him now. There was a cab rank near this corner, and often it was not deserted until past midnight. His premonition was well-founded, for the man in the raincoat lifted a hand as he came to the edge of the pavement, where the lights spilled over him yellowly, and the brightness of the black under his feet, glazed by the rain, redoubled their gleam with its baffling reflections. Here the Judge might have caught a glimpse of his face had he dared to come nearer, but instead all his attention was engaged in signalling up the next cab as soon as his quarry was in the act of opening the door of his.

'Please follow that taxi that just drove off,' said Mr Justice Manton to the indifferent ear that inclined to him from under a tilted cap.

He felt an odd sensation of distaste and self-consciousness, as though this rôle of hunter came too near to light fiction for his dignity and thrust him still more painfully out of his nature. The driver, too, slanted at him one of those looks of tolerant curiosity about the eccentric in which the Londoner is expert, and complied soothingly but contemptuously, with a heave of resigned shoulders, like one humouring a difficult child.

Now that he was back among a steady stream of traffic and lights, and the pavements had their fair number of people walking, he felt more acutely than ever the nightmare nature of his pursuit. When he looked back at his long and distinguished public career it appeared to him unreal and distorted, as though it had fallen out of focus, or he himself had become warped, and some monstrous transmutation would be needed ever to fit him into that background again. He kept his eyes fixed upon the car they were following, but no suspicion of pursuit seemed to have entered his quarry's mind, and there were taxis

enough threading the back streets to keep his own incon-
spicuous.

So intent was he upon his own inner experiences that
the part of London through which he was being led made
no impression upon his mind. They had left the
Cromwell Road, moving east towards Sloane Street
through quiet squares and residential streets, and were
just drawing into one more dignified green square of
trees exactly like the rest, when he thought with a shock
of amused recognition: 'He's taking me past my own
door!'

At that moment they were met by another taxi, just
driving round from their right and leaving the square by
the way they were entering. The Judge recognised the
number-plate with an exclamation of surprise, and
deeper within him a convulsion of foreboding.

'They're doubling back!'

'No, sir. 'E's empty. 'E's dropped 'is fare.'

The driver pulled up, looking round for further
instructions. Beyond the clump of trees, on the other side
of the square, a front door closed crisply. Mr Justice
Manton sat still, gazing in the direction of the sound,
while the quietness of Clevely Square came back to rest
slowly, like birds after a rifle shot. Then he said calmly:
'That's all right, thanks. I'll get out here.'

He paid off the taxi, and walked without hesitation
round the railed garden to his own front door. The face
of the house was dark, and as he let himself in there was
no sound but that of the cab driving away. No light on
the landing, no rustle of movement on the stairs. He
went up in the dark, one flight, two flights, three. On the

left, Margaret's room, empty and dark and neat. On the right, Charlie's.

He went in without knocking, and switched on the light. A startled little grunt from the bed greeted the sudden brightness, and Charlie's tousled head rolled on the pillow. His cheeks were flushed, his mouth soft like a sleepy child's. He parted his eyelids a little, protestingly, and muttered and blinked, rubbing the back of a hand over his eyes, then heaved himself over and buried his face in the pillow again to shut out the light. He looked unbearably young, and rash, and innocent.

The Judge looked from his tumbled bed to the accustomed untidiness of the room, the dinner-jacket hitched askew over the back of a chair, the socks and shoes shed over the carpet, the tie coiled upon the hearth-rug. It was all exactly as it always was; the boy had always defied anyone to reduce him or his works to conventional order.

His father, watching his sullen and charming sleep, thought: 'Perhaps, after all, I'm wrong!' He crossed the carpet gently, and Charlie sighed and opened his dazzled eyes again resignedly and muttered: 'What's the matter?' Then, consenting to awaken by degrees: 'Oh, hullo, Dad! What's wrong?' He yawned, rubbing his cheeks, and lay blinking lazily, and after a moment fell gradually into a dreamy smiling.

Mr Justice Manton stooped and picked up one of the discarded shoes. The sole was dark with moisture. He put his hand into the shoe and felt the toe, and the warmth of Charlie's foot was still there, the warmth of his own blood.

Charlie's head remained quiet upon the pillow, but

now his dark eyes had flared open to their widest and were following this gesture with extreme and motionless intelligence, and the smile had gone from the brilliant, tender, self-willed mouth.

The Judge dropped the shoe, and going to the wardrobe, opened the door. A soft brown hat rolled out at his feet. Beneath it lay a dark fawn raincoat, hurriedly bundled together, still damp with the soft rain. He picked it up and shook it out, and the right-hand pocket sagged heavily with the weight of the revolver.

When he turned back to the bed with the thing in his hand, Charlie was sitting up and putting back the disordered covers from him. His crumpled shirt, without collar and tie, opened upon his handsome brown throat. He swung his trousered legs out of bed, and sat there calmly, looking at his father. He no longer looked a child, much less a sleepy child. In the long, dark cheeks the familiar shadowy hollows quivered strangely with implications of both laughter and sorrow. The half-smiling lips drooped now, cased of any necessity for deception, a little tired, a little spiteful, a little affectionate.

'You *would* know!' he sighed, between chiding and sympathy. He reached out towards his jacket a hand which was almost perfectly steady, and took out his cigarette-case. 'What are you going to do now?' he asked, curious even in this moment, when respect and regret for the old man oppressed him almost as much as his weariness.

Mr Justice Manton crossed to the door, and carefully closed it. Then he came back to the bed, moving slowly and laboriously, suddenly a very old man. Groping clumsily, he laid the revolver upon the turned-back sheet beside his son's hand.

Charlie looked down at it for a moment, and then lifted to the stony old face above him, ravaged with grief, a soft, indulgent smile. He said with a slight shake of his head: 'I shan't need that.' He reached up a hand, and pulled gently at the Judge's sleeve. 'Sit down, Brutus!' he said comfortingly. 'There's no hurry now, I'm not going to run. Sit down, and I'll tell you all about it.'

Charlie came into Margaret's room in the morning, while she was still asleep. She awoke to the touch of lips upon hers, infinitely soft, and lay smiling with her eyes still closed, thinking of Malachi, and convinced that she was still dreaming. But when she finally looked up, the reluctant lids rolling back slowly from the dazed dark blue of her eyes, it was her cousin's face that was bending over her. He was smiling, and the only thing she found unusual about him was that he should bother to pay her such a visit at all, even if he was, as he said, going out of town. He was already dressed for travelling, and had his brief-case under his arm.

'Are you going to be away long?' she asked, frowning up at him through her sleepiness.

He said, the spark of wry mischief coming and going very briefly in his eyes: 'Not long. I shan't be back tonight, probably, but you may be hearing from me before the day's out.'

'And when you do come home, you'll rush in just in time to snatch a bath, and change, and rush out again as usual!'

'No,' said Charlie, smiling at her with a curious, intent gentleness, 'I promise you the next time I come home it'll be to stay.' He twisted his fingers in a curl of her hair, and tugged at it softly. 'You should talk! I heard you come in at nearly three o'clock this morning. No wonder you're still sleepy.'

'What brought you awake at three in the morning?' Filled with her own joy and longing to share it, she caught at his hand and clung to it for a moment. 'Charlie, something wonderful happened last night. You'll wish us luck, I know – I'm going to marry Malachi!'

'I'm not a bit surprised,' said Charlie sagely. 'I saw it coming.' He stooped and kissed her again, lightly upon the cheek. 'Congratulations! I hope you'll both be very happy.'

He looked back from the doorway as he was going, and said: 'Good-bye!' and it did not seem to her that the word had any unusual overtones, nor that anything of the Charlie she knew was missing from his light movements or his gay smile. Then the door closed on him, and she heard, from the contented margin of sleep, the sound of his footsteps as he ran down the stairs.

That was the last she ever saw of him.

The telephone call came early in the afternoon. Margaret was out with Malachi, and the Judge was alone when he took the call, which was as he would have chosen. He listened with a controlled face, and said at the end of the brief message: 'Thank you for telling me at once. I understand. I am coming down there myself, immediately.'

When he had replaced the receiver he sent for the housekeeper, who had been with him for many years. She found him already pulling on his greatcoat and gloves, and his authoritative manner had not changed in the least as he said to her:

93

'Mrs Platt, I have just had bad news. Mr Charles has had a crash with his car, on the road to Hastings. I am going down there straightaway, and when Miss Margaret comes in I don't want her to know that there is anything wrong. I'll talk to her myself when I come back, but until then I don't want her to worry. You had better tell her simply that I've been called away, and don't expect to be back until late this evening. I know I can leave her quite safely in your hands. Oh, and, Mrs Platt – if you could keep the evening papers out of her sight, it would be better.'

She might ask for them, of course, but he did not think it likely. Margaret's interest in the papers would not be very great tonight. The rendezvous was already past and fruitless in her eyes, and the presence of the young man Malachi would occupy all her thoughts and energies. The Judge had seen the print of last night's revelation in the radiance of her face. Everything else must have become very pale and far away; not even death can compete with love. No, Margaret would surely be safe.

The housekeeper, hovering, said distractedly: 'I hope Mr Charlie isn't badly hurt?'

Mr Justice Manton looked through her with fixed but quiet eyes, and said: 'Charlie is dead. It seems he crashed the car at high speed into a stone quarry beside the road. I'm going down there now to arrange about the inquest, and about bringing his body home.'

He sat bolt upright in the car behind his chauffeur throughout the journey; and when he came back, at about nine o'clock in the evening, his back was as straight and his voice as firm as ever, only his face had

94

drawn itself into tight lines of strain, as if flesh and skin had shrunk upon the bone, as if months of hunger and pain had been compressed into the few hours of his ordeal. His eyes had eaten half his face, and burned their way deeply into his head in great, gaunt hollows, but their expression was such that no one dared try to utter a word of condolence. They said afterwards that they had never guessed he thought so much of the boy.

He asked after Margaret, but she had gone out again with Malachi and was not yet home. The Judge, staring into a future he could no longer bear to prolong, felt a rush of relief and gratitude at not having to face her. He had meant to wait until Charlie was buried, but now he knew that he had not the strength to fulfil his obligations to Margaret, not face to face with her, never aloud. It was the first time in his life that he had admitted to himself that a plain duty might yet be something which could not be borne.

He shut himself into his study, sat down at his desk and began to write three long letters. The one for Margaret was the shortest of the three. There was so much to be explained, and courtesy demanded that no detail should be overlooked, to torment some equally meticulous mind later on.

Margaret and Malachi were in the St James's Theatre, hand in hand in the darkness and invulnerably happy in each other. In the porch of St Lucian Martyr in Kensington, another pair of lovers had just happened horribly upon Sir Robert Wyvern's body. Mr Justice Manton sat at his desk, punctilious to the last, drawing together the strands of the Stevenson case, his patrician profile so worn and shrunken with pain that he might have been already a dead man. The last hours of his life he spent upon his passion, which was justice.

Malachi brought Margaret back before half-past eleven that night, because she wished to present him at once to her uncle and announce their engagement. It seemed to him that half-past eleven might be regarded as a rather late hour for such family ordeals, but Margaret over-ruled his protests and towed him into the house by the hand.

'Of course he'll still be up, he never goes to bed before midnight. And the ice will be broken then, and in any case at this hour you needn't stay long. I believe you're scared of him,' she said, looking up into his face as she switched on more lights in the hall.

'Aren't most people? *You* are!' said Malachi provoca-tively.

She smiled, but rather thoughtfully. 'Not scared, exactly, but I could never get any nearer to him. I can't say I've ever known him – really known him. Nobody does, unless it's Charlie, and they've gone their own ways since long before I came here to live.'

She threw open the door of the drawing-room, but it was empty and dark, and the fire was almost out. 'He must be up in his study. Let's go up to him.'

They climbed the first flight of stairs hand in hand, and saw together the thin line of brightness under the study door; but when Margaret tapped confidently on the panels and made to go in, the door resisted her. She looked round at Malachi in surprise: 'It's locked! I never knew him do that before.'

She raised her voice, and called cheerfully: 'Uncle

John, can I come in? I want to talk to you.'

The silence after her voice was like a blow. Malachi, who had been about to protest once again that they should postpone the interview and not disturb an old man at this time of night, let the words die in his mouth. Margaret's face had changed, sharpening into serious anxiety. 'There must be something wrong. Malachi, I don't like this!'

'He may have fallen asleep,' said Malachi sensibly.

'He doesn't sleep like this – he'd have heard me.' But she knocked again on the door, and called again: 'Uncle John, are you all right? Please let me in – it's Margaret!'

After every knock, every call, the silence fell back stonily. She turned and shut her hands on Malachi's arm tightly. 'Malachi, I'm afraid! Something's happened to him!'

'Don't be silly, what could happen to him? You don't even know that he's there at all. He may have forgotten to put the light out.'

'Then why should he lock the door? He never does keep it locked. Malachi, there *is* something wrong. You ask what could happen to him. But something happened to the foreman of the jury, didn't it?'

'Now you're being absurd.' Malachi's voice was peremptory, as if to a potential case of hysteria, but Margaret, calm as she was, had no energy to spare for resenting his tone. 'If a locked door can start you back to all that nonsense—' It was the first time the case had been so much as mentioned between them all that day.

'One locked door may not be much,' said Margaret. 'But come into the library. There's a way through from there into the study, too. Let's see if that's locked.'

97

*　*　*

This time it was Malachi who put his hand to it, and then the weight of his shoulder. It resisted him solidly. The silence in the sealed study prolonged itself levelly, inhumanly. It no longer seemed possible to him that anyone could be in there, and sleep through the growing storm of their uneasiness.

'He *is* there,' said Margaret with absolute conviction.

'Would there be another key? To either of the doors?'

'Mrs Platt might have one, I don't know. Shall I go and wake her?'

'Yes,' said Malachi, swallowing hard, 'I think perhaps you'd better.' It was three flights up, and the errand might keep her away for ten minutes or more, as well as providing another woman to bear her company in whatever revelation was to come. He waited until she was on the stairs, and then went to the long windows of the library, and let himself out between the heavy burgundy curtains, on to a narrow stone balcony.

It did not reach the window of the room next door, but that window was identical with this one, and the distance between the two low stone balustrades was not more than two feet. He negotiated it easily, and tried the catch of the window, but it was fastened, and the glass was closely curtained within, so that only a glow of wine-coloured light came through. He hesitated for a moment, but, remembering Margaret, put away his doubts and, muffling his fist in his sleeve, smashed it through the glass beside the catch and let himself into the room with fragments of glass glittering like frost on his coat. He parted the curtains with a hand suddenly reluctant, and would have given anything to be absolved from the necessity: but someone had to venture, and it seemed to have become his responsibility. In the end it was with a lunge and a gulp that he passed through into the light.

Mr Justice Manton was still at his desk, lying forward over it almost as if in sleep; but the awkward fall of his left hand and arm, sprawled under his head, had none of the ease of sleep, and only his right hand, fallen half-open beside him on the blotter, kept its appearance of life and competence to the end. The revolver, the queer lump of the silencer clipping the barrel, rested naturally in the relaxed fingers, as if he had been used to handling such weapons, though until he had taken it from Charlie's pocket he had never so much as held one in his hand before.

He had made sure of suppressing the evening papers, and also extended a last courtesy to Mrs Platt, by spreading the *Gazette* and its fellow where his head would come to rest. The act conveyed to Malachi more about Mr Justice Manton than he had ever understood until this moment. Three sealed and addressed letters, all in the same strong Gothic hand, he had placed on the most distant corner of the desk, with the same consideration. It was as well, for the revolver was a heavy job, and had made a hideous mess. But the letters were clean. Malachi put out a hand which was perceptibly shaking, and took the one which was addressed to Margaret. The others seemed to be for the coroner and the police respectively. He knew he ought not to touch anything, but the old man had meant Margaret to have the letter, and it was hers, and – they could run him in for it if they liked – he was damned if she should have to wait for it.

He felt a wave of nausea rising in him, and fought it down doggedly. The sound of women's voices in the library sent him flying to that door, but the key was in the lock there, so they could not get in, even if they had another key. He spoke quickly, before he let himself out to rejoin them, because a movement within there might well be misinterpreted unless he identified himself at once.

'Margaret, I'm here. It's me, Malachi – I'm coming out.'

She said, with a laugh which was as near hysteria as it was in her nature to come: 'My God, we thought we'd lost you, too!'

He turned the key warily, and slid through the door and closed it quickly behind him. She confronted him large-eyed and pale, the older woman at her elbow, in a long woollen housecoat.

'Was there another key?'

'No, only those in the doors. How did you get in? Malachi, you're hurt!' She caught at the sleeve of his jacket and, pushing it up from the wrist, displayed the single long scratch where the glass had penetrated; but he put her off gently.

'No, that's nothing. I climbed over by the two balconies, and had to break the glass to get in.' He relocked the door and put the key thankfully into his pocket. 'We've got trouble, Margaret.'

The 'we' was meant to have its effect on her, and indeed she received it with gratitude, surrendering herself to his arm as he led her away from the door.

'Will you stay here with Mrs Platt, while I do some telephoning? Then I've got something to give you.' The silent questioning of her eyes, wildly intelligent, assured him that she was feeling her way so near the truth that he might as well put it into words. 'Yes, he's in there. You were right, something bad did happen to him. He's dead, Margaret. I've got to call the police.'

'The police?' she said in a whisper. It was not she, but the housekeeper, who had broken into disordered tears.

'He shot himself,' said Malachi, so gently that the words seemed to have lost all their impact, and sank into her consciousness very gradually. 'He left letters, Margaret. I don't know why he did it, but it was quite deliberate. Here, this is for you.'

She took it automatically, but for a long minute did not look at it. She found, somewhere in her, the faint shadow of a smile with which to comfort Malachi, whose pain for her was as yet the only pain she felt at all. 'All right – yes, I understand. I'm quite all right, Malachi, don't worry about me. You could telephone from—'

She remembered in time that the only telephone up here was on her uncle's desk, and turned her head away with a gesture of distress which he chose not to see, because any responsive distress on his part might have broken her.

'I'll go down,' he said, 'and leave the door unfastened for them. You stay here and take care of Mrs Platt. I'll be very quick.'

At least he knew she could not get into the study. He heard them talking spasmodically as he ran down the stairs, the housekeeper's voice shattered with tears.

Margaret took the older woman by the arm, and led her to a chair and sat beside her. 'Did you know this might happen? Did anything happen today, to make you think a

101

thing like this was possible?' For it seemed to her that this grief had little surprise in it.

'He told me not to say anything to you,' whispered Mrs Platt, between her sobs. 'He said he'd tell you himself, so I never said a word this evening. But by the time he came home you were out again. I thought he'd be waiting up to see you, because he came into his study here and said he wasn't to be disturbed unless you came in. So I had to leave him to take care of everything himself. But I never thought of him doing a thing like that! Still, after what's happened, you can understand it—'

'What has happened? What is it I wasn't to be told?'

Mrs Platt lifted a face of ravaged despair. 'It's Mr Charlie. He hoped you wouldn't see the papers, to read about it like that, without any warning. Mr Charlie had a smash with his car, this morning. The police down in Sussex telephoned the Judge, and he went down there, but I wasn't to tell you the reason. I ought to have thought of this – you could see it in his face when he came back, but I never realised.'

'Are you trying to tell me,' asked Margaret gently, 'that Charlie's dead too?' She felt nothing yet except a coldness, such as she supposed falls on the senses when something too large and grotesque for belief confronts and challenges them.

'He was killed outright. The car was all smashed up, he ran it into a stone quarry, the Judge said.' Her tears had calmed her, now that the worst was told and Margaret sat so still and composed under the burden. 'I could hardly believe it was happening, he was so quiet about it. You'd have thought he'd been preparing himself for news like that – really, you'd almost have thought he was expecting it.'

It was then that Margaret felt the light, astonishing kiss once more upon her lips, and saw for an instant Charlie's face hovering close above her just-opened eyes, out of focus, plaintively smiling. She heard again the soft, light tones of his voice, still playful in farewell, explaining that, though he would not be back that night, it would not be long before he came home, and that when he came home this time, it would be to stay. She heard his 'Goodbye!' which had seemed to her to hold no particular solemnity of leave-taking; it was poignant and final now in the ears of her memory. How could she have let such a visitation, such a valediction, pass without question? How was it she had not realised what lay behind it? Yes, the old man had been expecting it. He had known it was coming. So had his son. Something like this resolute and violent death had been agreed between them.

So now, though she did not understand the details of the dénouement, she recognised its force and finality. The Judge had been summoned to a tribunal, and he was gone to keep his appointment, in the only way it could be kept. Charlie, who had never been threatened by name, was gone with him. Had not one nameless person also been called with the rest of the guilty?

The last thing she had said to Malachi about the Stevenson case, last night as they walked home together tranquilly in the small hours after the rain had ceased, was: 'And now, after all, I suppose we shall never know who did it!'

She had spoken too soon, it seemed; she knew now, only too well, who had killed Zoë Trevor.

* * *

The detective-inspector looked at the unopened letter Margaret was holding out to him, and shook his head gently.

'I don't think we shall have to make use of that, Miss Manton, since you can verify the handwriting. They're all three his, obviously. And he's told us everything we're going to need, in detail. A very clear statement. This one – no, that's yours.' He rose and turned towards the closed door of the study, behind which the doctor and a sergeant were already at work. Privately he had warned Malachi that they would have to take away the old man's body for a more thorough examination. They wanted to extract the bullet, which was deeply embedded; but there was no need to pass on these thoughts to Margaret. 'I'm afraid we shall be some time. We'll try not to be more noticeable than we have to. If I were you, I should try to get some rest.'

Margaret looked up, hollow-eyed with shock, from the depths of the big chair in which she sat, and said in a low but level voice: 'I'm quite all right, thank you. Please go ahead.'

Mrs Platt had been sent back to bed with a sedative, under the doctor's orders, as soon as her own part of the story had been told. Margaret and Malachi were alone in the library now. He came and sat down on the arm of her chair and embraced her shoulders. They read the Judge's last letter together.

MY DEAR MARGARET,
   By the time you receive this I shall be already dead, and unable to apologise in person for leaving

104

you alone to face so terrible a series of discoveries. I can only ask you to forgive me for what will seem to you a betrayal, but I find I am not so strong as I had believed, and what I have to tell you is more mercifully said in this way, without the distress of another meeting.

You will know by now that Charlie is dead. I had intended to break that news to you myself, for I know that you were very fond of him, as indeed he was of you; but, apart from the fact that cowardice prompts me to take this easier way, I find myself believing also, rightly or wrongly, that it is a matter of urgency that I should lose no time in rejoining my son. If any continued travelling awaits us, I should like to think that we may undertake it in company; and that is why I am in so unseemly a hurry to overtake him.

You will forgive me if I do not again go into details. I have left a full account for the police of everything that has happened. But I must tell you that owing to observations I made during the last two days, both of your behaviour and of Sir Robert Wyvern's, I felt it incumbent upon me to be present at the proposed meeting at St Lucian's Church last night. I was already convinced that some interested person, most probably you, my dear Margaret, was trying to make the supposed murderer break cover by means of this appointment; and my absolute conviction that we had already done justice in that case had already been shaken, not by the accidental death of the foreman of the jury so much as by some inward uneasiness within myself, of which

I think Robert's fatalism was the earliest source. It seemed to me that if there really did exist some person who could be alarmed by the threat of revelations regarding Zoë Trevor's stolen jewellery, that person could be none other than the murderer, and we had indeed destroyed an innocent man. You will understand, therefore, that I had to be present.

I was in hiding on the scene when you came and when you were startled into flight, and I have seen in your bearing today that that particular encounter did not belong in the orbit of this tragic evil in which the rest of us are caught. My only consolation in leaving you like this is my conviction that I leave you to a happiness which cannot always be shadowed by the manner of my departure.

After you left, I continued to wait, and two men came singly to the church and met there. One of them, whom I knew afterwards to be Robert, flashed a torch in the other one's face and clearly recognised him, though I myself did not have the opportunity at that time of seeing him clearly. Robert was thereupon shot down immediately by the other man, who then made his escape, and whom I followed from the scene. It was clear to me then that this was the murderer. He had come for the sole purpose of killing the person who, as he supposed, could incriminate him. There had been almost no noise throughout, and the revolver was silenced. I was sorry to have to leave poor Robert like that, but he was already dead, and my duty was quite clear to me.

I followed the murderer, and he led me to my own house. The clothes my son had been wearing I recovered from his wardrobe in his presence. He must have received a mortal shock when he heard me open and close the front door so promptly upon his own entry. The revolver also I took from him, and after my death it will come, with all the rest of the vital evidence, into the hands of the police.

It is characteristic of my son Charlie that since he began to consider himself a man, which he did very early, he has asked no favours nor concessions of me, of any other person, or of life. He grew too early and too easily into a celebrity in warfare, and reached a height of accomplishment in this dubious line which has debarred him from all achievement in less exciting fields since. What he needed to while away the remainder of a deflowered life he considered it his natural part to take, never to ask for. He was self supporting, emotionally as well as in every other way. The world owed him whatever he could take from it. Yet you have reason, I think, to know as well as I do that he could be moved to an equally staggering generosity. It is true that probably no one in the world but himself was quite real to him, but he had moments of realisation when they became real, and then he could make large and terrible gestures in celebration of his vision.

I think that is how Zoë came to die. He told me so, and since he was asking nothing of me, neither silence nor help, I see no reason to disbelieve what he said.

It seems there has never been a time when

Charlie was not in debt. He lived an expensive life, and had some exacting friends. That I should know nothing of his difficulties is not so surprising as it may seem; he would no more have thought of coming to me for money than to a stranger in the street. It was his part to get what he needed by his own initiative. There may have been some questionable transactions earlier, but certainly at the time when he met Zoë Trevor again after a long estrangement he was deep in debt and being pressed for settlement by some dangerous friends. You may know that after his demobilisation he had been one of the procession of Zoë's young admirers. I knew it myself, but did not suppose, nor indeed did he, that he had been more important in that company than any of the others. It was he who had been the first to abandon the association, but since Zoë was no more real to him than the rest of us, except in glimpses, it had not occurred to him that she might have suffered by his defection.

When by chance they were thrown together again, she showed that she was willing to renew the acquaintance on the old terms. He says freely that when he consented to go to her house that night, he went to rob her. She was notoriously casual with her money; there were often large untraceable sums in the house, apart from valuables. If he had asked her for a loan to tide him over his difficulties, she would probably have given it to him – you remember the little debts of Louis Stevenson? – but Charlie never asked for things. It was outside his code. He intended to take, and she had then the remedy of setting the police on him if she chose. Watching her and wondering whether she would do so would probably have afforded him a kind of stimulation which he constantly needed. But what he does say is that he did not, at that time, intend to kill her.

When he went in to her, he says, he had a shock. She had made every effort to turn back time for him, to leap back across the six years during which they had hardly met. She wore the dress she had often worn for him then. They dined together, and his uneasiness became intense, because her pleasure in him was distressing to that unwillingness he had to be touched, to have other people's delight and pain encroach upon his singleness. At his suggestion they washed-up afterwards, and she cleared everything away, thus eliminating most of the traces of his visit. Then they went into the room where she was afterwards found dead. She was lying upon the settee, and he – it was expected of him – sat down beside her and embraced her.

In the kiss he suffered one of those moments of enlightenment, and she became a person. He says that he felt her love for him pass into his mind like fire. It had not occurred to him that Zoë could love. She told him that he was her life, and without him she had been in a kind of death which did not preclude suffering. He says that he knew it was true, and that her joy was more than he could bear. He foresaw in his heart her situation when she found that he had been making a fool of her, and had come not because he loved her, but because he

109

needed her money. What was he to do? He could not rob her and abandon her to such a terrible disillusionment, but neither could he satisfy her by loving her, for he loved no one but himself. Nor was he prepared to withdraw from the situation and abandon his purpose, which would now neither serve him nor preserve her. He says that he could see no way out but to bestow on her one moment at least of triumph and happiness, and destroy her at the height of it. It seemed to him the lesser cruelty.

And that is why he killed her, and killed her as he did. When she was dead, he erased the remaining traces of his presence, took all the money and jewellery he could find in the house, and left. With the money he paid off the most pressing of his debts, and he has since disposed of three small pieces of jewellery, but the rest will in due course be restored intact to Zoë's heirs.

On leaving the theatre at which he spent the later part of that evening, he was robbed, somewhere in the street, of two small items. But of this incident you know already.

Having told me this story, Charlie agreed with me quite simply that he had lost the game and his life was forfeit, and of course he did not ask me to take any other view. He asked for nothing; that was not his habit. He told me that he would make his own exit in his own way, but promised not to delay it beyond tonight. This bargain, to which I had no right to agree, I nevertheless accepted. He has kept his part of it; but I do not think he realised that I meant to go with him. I do so, not entirely because my own honour is also at stake, and my own life forfeit, but chiefly because I wish to accompany my son to whatever further experience may be waiting for him. And if there is nothing further, I prefer to end with him.

I had thought to leave behind me his own statement of his motives and actions, but he refused to go to so much trouble, saying that he was content to leave the reporting to me, because I should be scrupulously just to everybody. He says too, though on this point he may be deluding himself, that he had not reconciled himself to letting Stevenson die in his place, and, but for the decision of that unfortunate man to shorten the ordeal, he would have made some attempt to extricate him from his unhappy situation. I have said, I do not know how much value to attach to this expressed intention; but I do believe that he himself believed it to be true, for he had no possible motive for lying to me.

Lastly, Margaret, I am exercised in mind at the thought of what will follow my death; and though I see no way of convincing the world, I beg you, at least, most solemnly to accept my assurance that we have none of us been hounded to our deaths by the sick fancies of a much-wronged man. We are the victims of no one but ourselves. It is our own actions, not the curses of others, which pursue us. The Assize of the Dying has its court in the mind, and we are our own accusers.

I hope that you will forgive me soon, and in the

course of time forget, if not me, at least the discourtesy of my abrupt departure. My warmest good wishes remain with you for the future.

Your affectionate uncle,

JOHN MANTON.

She folded the precise sheets carefully, and put them back into the envelope. Suddenly she could not see the laborious movements of her own hands for the dazzle of tears, and Malachi, observing their lame fumblings, took the letter from her and lifted her impetuously into his arms.

'We'll never touch the jewellery, you needn't even see it! We'll sell the wretched stuff, and give the money away. We'll sell up the house in Hampstead, and get out of here for good. In Canada you'll soon forget all this. It's done and done with, you won't be able to remember it there. That's another country, Margaret, and another life. You'll like it – I'll make you happy—'

She was dazed with weariness and tension, and, held fast in his arms, clinging to him gratefully, she let her senses drown in the sound of his voice whispering passionate reassurances against her cheek. So she never heard the other door of the study open, and the slow procession of footsteps pass along the landing to the stairs, as the stretcher-men carried Mr Justice Manton away.

AUNT HELEN

Chapter 1

It was turning out exactly like all the other abortive attempts to get Uncle Philip to see reason. He should have known better than to expect anything else. It had begun with a kind of forbearing tolerance, and was ending in anger. He stood with his shoulder turned on the older man, and stared hard out of the window at the delectable Easter greens of Helen's garden, and the greenish silvery curve of the river bearing round towards the mill-wheel, but what he was seeing was the dwindling week of grace Lawson had allowed him in which to raise his share of the capital, and the priceless opportunity, slippery as silk and delicate as glass, falling through his impotent fingers for ever. He was being treated like an irresponsible child, though it was the whole course of his life that was at stake. He knew what he was about, he was as good a judge of a speculation as Philip, any day. He was twenty-two, and it was his money, and he wanted and needed it now, not in three years' time, and it was damned unfair that Philip should be able to prevent him from handling it.

He said as much, the words bursting out of his lips furiously: 'I'm not a child! I'm twenty-two!'

'I'm glad you reminded me, boyo,' said Philip, in that

aggravatingly sweet and buoyant voice of his, 'before I forgot myself, and took action that wouldn't sort at all with the dignity of your years. And if I were you I'd be off now, before the exact figure slips my mind again. It's the tantrums that take me back – first time bad luck ever dumped you in my lap you were purple in the face with temper – just like you are now!'

Bill Grant was startled into flashing one indignant glance towards the mirror that hung beside the window, and realised his folly and snatched his gaze away too late to avert the quiet chuckle with which his uncle scored up the point. He repeated doggedly: 'I'm of age, and it's my money.'

'It's your money, all right, and it's my job to see that it's still there for you when you're twenty-five. And it's going to be there, make no mistake about that.'

'But this opportunity won't be there, and you know it. I've told you over and over—'

'You have, Bill, you have, I grant you that. It isn't for want of hearing the facts I'm still saying no.' Philip watched the boy's sullen and desperate face impatiently, keeping the place in his half-corrected proof with a long forefinger. Two years of conscription did this sort of thing to even the best-balanced of young men, and he was willing to bear with the agonies of re-adjustment with a certain degree of philosophy, even with some sympathy. Not, however, to the extent of letting the young idiot ruin himself to line the pockets of a smooth character like this Lawson of his. 'Your mother, bless her heart, must have had a premonition about you. Not that you'll necessarily stop being a mug when you reach twenty-five, but one has to let go the strings some time. You can

116

buy gold bricks on your twenty-fifth birthday, not before. The last thing I ever wanted was to act as trustee for anyone, let alone a pig-headed brat like you, but since I got the job whether I wanted it or not, by God, I'm going to do it properly. I don't like your prospective partner, boyo, I don't like his proposition, and I don't like your chances of being solvent at twenty-three if I let you get your hands on your capital now. And that's my last word.'

'I believe you *want* to ruin my life!' burst out Bill. 'But I'll get the money yet, in spite of you!'

Philip's incipient irritation was quite disarmed by this naïveté, and he broke into that sudden and impish smile which was as disconcerting on his grave face as laughter on the dark, disillusioned and sorrowful countenance of the Merry Monarch; whom, so he had often been told, he somewhat resembled. 'Oh, come!' he said reproachfully, 'I could write you better lines than that, myself! But if that's the level on which you want to play the scene, I can only come back with: Over my dead body!'

'And that could be arranged, too!' said Bill, flushed and scowling, and ready to say anything to establish the extremity of his desperation. He had been trying all his life to impress Uncle Philip with his reality and stature as a person, and never succeeded yet, but he could not stop believing that he would manage it some day. The result, now as always, was disastrous. Philip's handsome, shaggy, greying head went back delightedly, and he shouted with laughter, snatching his finger out of the proof, and pushing it skidding away across the desk.

'Oh, Bill, Bill, my soul, you make me feel young again! What are you proposing? – a duel? – or a cup of cold poison? You'd take care of Helen afterwards, wouldn't you? Only don't be too sure she'd let you have your own way about the money – you don't know her as well as you think you do.'

Bill wrenched himself away from the window and flung out of the room, scarlet to the forehead with shame at his own inadequacy and rage for his wrongs. When Philip stopped being angry and began to laugh he knew he was finished; there was nothing he could do now to get himself taken seriously. And those Renauds would be in the house all the week-end, and there would be precious few opportunities to get Philip alone again and try to make a better job of it. And he had only five days left to realise the money, if he wanted to go with Lawson to Canada. He slammed the door of Philip's study behind him as a small sop to the fever of spite that filled him, and plunged down the stairs into the great hall of the millhouse, where the early evening shadows were lengthening. Mary was arranging some fresh flowers in a big silver bowl for the dinner-table. She gave him a quick glance as he passed her and went out into the garden, noted the flushed face and scowling brows, and the tremors of mortification that wrenched at his lips, and wisely made no attempt to stop or speak to him. He was on his way to Helen, of course. Whenever he felt like that – and there was no denying he was being a very difficult boy since he'd come out of the army – he always made a bee-line for Helen, and she always knew what to say to him.

Helen was just coming over the pack-bridge which crossed the river at the end of the garden, and provided the quickest way to and from the village. The sound of the mill-race made a constant throbbing there, and the dark coppices closed in to the water, and coloured its fast, still depths olive-green. The huge, rough stones of the bridge, yellow with moss, had no parapets; by night it was better to go round, unless you knew the spot very well, but Helen always used this route, by daylight or darkness. No one knew it as she did. She had persuaded Philip to buy Hugonin's Mill as a wedding present for her, and she had made it gradually into the lovely place it was now, practically with her own hands. Now it starred as the subject of articles in all the home-making magazines, and had been painted by more artists than Bill could remember. Wherever Helen put her gentle fingerprint on a place or a person, it became the mark of quality and grace. Bill hoped humbly that some day people would be able to recognise even in him that he was Helen's work.

She was forty-five, but she still looked less than thirty, slender as a girl, and fair as a yellow rose. Her beauty was the lasting kind, because so much of it was invisible to the eye but only implied, in the tenderness of the dreaming mouth and the soft attentiveness of her glance, in the unfailing tranquillity of her movements and the beautiful repose of her stillness. She had brought him up from the age of seven, when she married his uncle and guardian, and he was still astonished and grateful every time he saw her afresh after half an hour's absence. A good thing for the child, people had said fervently – and unwisely they had said it all too often in the child's sharp and intelligent hearing – when Helen took over both the uncle and the nephew, otherwise who knew how the boy might have turned out under Philip Greville's unregenerate influence? But with Helen any child was safe. And any man, too, it seemed. The little pitcher with long ears had spent a great many hours of his childhood working out all the implications of the things he over-heard, and he was well aware that according to the general opinion Helen had made a new and far better man of Philip. But he wasn't as surprised as they seemed to be about that, because he lived with Helen, too, and he knew that loving her could change anyone.

She let him take the shopping basket from her, and laid a cool finger against his still suffused cheek. He didn't turn his face away from her; it was never necessary to hide anything from Helen.

'You've been teasing Philip again! Silly child, I warned you he was involved with proofs and wanted to get them away. Which of you have I to be nice to this time?'

'Me! He won, hands down. And I'm no forrarder!' It was odd that he never minded being called a silly child by her, though he hated it when Philip so much as implied a want of years or sense in him. 'Oh, Helen, do help me to make him see reason! He doesn't listen to me, but he will to you. I've only got a few days left, and then I'm sunk. It's the sort of chance that comes only once in a lifetime. If I miss it I can never hope for another.'

She took his arm, and turned him gently to face her. 'Darling, do you want so much to leave us?'

'No, I – Yes, I suppose I do. But it isn't like that! I have to launch out for myself some time, haven't I? I don't want to leave *you* – how could I? – but some day I've got to. And I do want to set up for myself and manage my own life. Everybody wants that.'

'And Philip wants it for you, Bill, believe me, he does. Only he distrusts this project, and doesn't want you to go into it and then be disappointed.'

'I shan't be disappointed. I tell you, the thing's all right, Lawson's all right, Philip's making a frightful mistake, and I'm the one who's going to suffer for it. And it's my money, I've a right to it, haven't I? *You'd* let me have it, if it was in your hands, wouldn't you?'

'Oh, Bill, my dear, how can I say? I should want to know all about the thing before I gave in – for your sake, of course I should. And I'm not clever about business. I'm glad it's Phil who has the decision, and not me.'

'But you *would* give in,' persisted Bill with certainty. 'You wouldn't be able to go on flatly saying no to me. *You* wouldn't make me angry. I shouldn't make a fool of myself with *you*. I always do with him.'

She said with a quiet smile: 'You make too much of it when you fall out with him. You're far too alike to get on together very smoothly. Only promise me, darling, to leave him alone now, or you'll only make things worse. He had a lot of work to finish – and now the Renauds coming for the week-end, and he'll have to be sociable, too.'

'But I can't let it go at that,' protested Bill, aghast. 'I've *got* to try again. Unless *you'd* talk to him for me! Would you? Helen, would you? Helen, *please*!' He shut his arms round her and hugged her, cajoling her as shamelessly as he had done at seven years old. 'It's terribly important to me, you don't know how much it means. Oh, Helen, will you?'

'I don't promise to ask him to do what you want. Remember that! But I promise I'll talk it over with him, and try to advise him to let you have the money, if I think it justified – *if* I think it justified, I said. But only if you're good, and let him alone, and make yourself useful with the guests tonight.' She gasped and laughed, holding him off breathlessly. 'Well, that's a better face than you were wearing five minutes ago, at any rate. If you continue to improve, at least you'll be fit to appear in company without frightening the Renauds out of the house. It shouldn't be any hardship to be nice to the lady – she's very beautiful.'

Helen was the most outspoken of women in recognising beauty in others. Perhaps the reason she had always given him such a feeling of security was because she herself was so secure. Perversely, and on an impulse he instantly regretted bitterly, he said: 'Mrs Renaud is an old flame of Philip's – did you know?'

Her laughter, as radiant as it was quiet, dispersed the sudden sense of shock he had felt at his own spurt of mischief. Of course she knew! Was there anything to be known about Philip that she didn't know? And for the best of reasons, because Philip himself had no secrets from her.

'What an unpleasantly knowing child you must have been,' she said smiling, 'before I took you in hand. There was a time when your uncle was virtually a mass of flames – yes, I know. You can't expect that to surprise me – I found him attractive, too.'

'Sorry, darling! You ought to box my ears when I say things like that. But I really did wonder why you invited them. I mean – well, I don't suppose Renaud knows, and it could be a little awkward, couldn't it?'

'Actually, Estelle did the inviting practically single-handed. She made it so plain what she wanted that I was too feeble to pretend not to understand. But I don't suppose there'll be the slightest awkwardness. Why should there? It's a very long time ago.'

A very long time ago! Fifteen years of a fabulous marriage separated Helen from any shadow of anxiety on Estelle Renaud's account, even supposing she had ever been capable of feeling such anxiety. And of course she never had.

'They'll be here in about half an hour,' she said. 'Come and help me to put my music ready for tomorrow night, then I shan't have to bother about it later.'

'And you won't forget your promise?' he asked, falling into step beside her, almost comforted.

'Do I usually forget my promises?'

Between the soup and the coffee a subtle change had taken place in Estelle's thoughts and preoccupations at Helen's table. At first she had been thinking, as she took stock of Philip's spare profile by leisurely glances: 'He looks his age!' But by the end of the meal she was wondering: 'Does he think I look mine?' It was not that the affair had as yet any particular importance for her. It was rather that she felt a totally unexpected curiosity about this miraculous pairing, which had lasted fifteen years in the teeth of all probability, and looked, at least to outward view, proof against the ravages of fifteen more. The constancy of the naturally inconstant has always a perverse challenge about it, and Don Juan married is twice as attractive as Don Juan single. But can you be as curious as that about a person without risking a more dangerous kind of interest?

He looked as she would have expected Philip to look after so long an interval, handsome and distinguished in his middle-aged domesticity, with an attractive frosting of grey in his thick hair, but brows and lashes as black as ever, and lean dark cheeks quick with tremors of sensibility still, signalling his private moments of amusement very clearly for one who knew the signs. Yes, he looked his age, but his age became him. And she? She was forty-seven. Did he still think her beautiful? She pushed the momentary hypocrisy away from her in disgust, for she knew perfectly well that she was beautiful, and that he was far too much of an artist not to appreciate her, however inconvenient she might be as a reminder of the past. She was tall and resplendent, and not afraid of her opulent colouring, her red-gold hair and violet eyes; and thinking back pleasurably to those old days when they had been together, she found herself his match still.

They had sown wild oats lavishly in those days and it had not troubled her at all to be one of a joyous procession of women in his life, nor had she found his manner of scattering his talents at all wasteful, nor his wild reputation a reproach to her equally prodigal spirit. Strange how differently two women could look at the same man! She gazed thoughtfully at Helen across the table, marking the fair and delicate loveliness, the measured movements, the singular appropriateness of every word and every silence, every gesture and every stillness. This was the woman he'd gone so far as to marry. It was the first opportunity Estelle had ever had to observe her closely. This woman had transformed not only his state but his life. What had not troubled Estelle was anathema to her; she could not allow Philip to continue to throw his many gifts broadcast like largesse, making nothing of them, getting nothing out of them, burning himself out unprofitably. She had turned him into a model husband, faithful without question, industrious, disciplined, canalising his powers into the books which had made a name for him in the world – probably the most elegant and scholarly thrillers in the English language. Minor achievements, maybe, but very respectable achievements, all the same. He had a reputation in literary circles now. He had money, too, which was an asset not to be despised. Estelle knew all about that; she had married for money, once her early fling was over. Bohemianism for life was a luxury she could not afford.

She looked at her husband, being attentive to Helen there on the opposite side of the table. Gerard was nearly sixty, and developing the heavy, drooping fleshiness of the sedentary business-man, the penalty of his capacity for making money; but she certainly couldn't complain that he hadn't kept his side of the bargain. There was more money than even she could ever spend. She had never tried to alter him, when she finally decided, seven years ago now, that it was time to settle down and turn her assets to lasting account. No, it took a different kind of arrogance from hers, to assume that you could take a man and make him over into a show-piece, just as easily as you could do the same efficient job on Hugonin's Mill.

And it might have worked, she thought, watching Gerard's thick, pale neck crease as he bent over Helen, if he hadn't been such a bore. Let's face it, boredom starts more trouble than malice does. If he hadn't been so dull I might never have invited the two of us down here for Easter; we should just have exchanged a few politenesses that evening we met so unexpectedly in the foyer of the theatre, and parted without leaving any loose ends. But I was spoiling for something to do, and there was Philip, and I just felt it would be a change. And perhaps I wanted to see if there was anything left that would blow up into a flame again – just to keep my hand in. And now I only want – Well, what do I want? I don't know yet. I can't be sure.

'I've often heard you broadcast, Mrs Greville,' Gerard was saying. 'You gave a Schubert recital one night last autumn – I admired your singing of "Gretchen" very much.'

'Oh, did you hear that? I don't really sing Schubert well, I wasn't altogether happy about it. I prefer singing Mozart, myself – maybe I need the greater discipline.'

'Helen has a twenty-minute TV recital tomorrow night,' said Philip proudly. 'Her own loves this time – Mozart and Bach.'

'I feel very guilty about abandoning you all for the day,' said Helen, with her tender and brilliant smile, 'but I can hardly back out of it. And it isn't often they give me the chance to make up a whole programme of the items I like best. On Good Friday I can get away with it, you see.'

'Your concerts during the year are distressingly few, though, if I may say so.' Gerard could always talk music, it was one more of his interests which Estelle did not share. 'We should like to hear much more of you.'

'Helen has to be rather careful how much she under-takes,' Philip explained for her. 'She has a heart condition that keeps her from exerting herself too much. And she finds broadcasting less demanding than concert appearances.'

'Less tiring, at any rate,' said Helen, with a deprecating frown and a quick smile in her husband's direction. 'No, don't feel concerned about me, please, Mr Renaud. Phil is making too much of it. I'm not ill, you know, I'm just under supervision, and ordered to take things easy. And that suits my inclinations very well, as a matter of fact. This will be my first appearance on television, though; I'm quite looking forward to it. Personally, I've never thought that it was a medium very suited to song recitals, I must admit.'

'In this particular case,' said Gerard gallantly, 'I must disagree. Both senses will share the same delight.'

Heavy-handed, thought Estelle, a connoisseur of compliments. But quite in the character of this house. They all adore her. That dim elder sister of Phil's, who used to hang around in the old day simply because of the baby – if you ask me, it's because of Helen she hangs around now, she always disapproved of Philip, though I dare say the new model's more to her taste than the old one. And the boy himself, it's easy to see what he thinks of Auntie. Been in love with her, I should judge, since he was about ten, only luckily he's much too simple to have the least notion what ails him. All he needs, when he fixes his eyes on her like that, is a lighted candle and a smell of incense. What he really needs, of course, is a girl. And Philip – Philip is a dead duck. He's hers body and soul. Unless, of course – unless—

It was at that moment that Philip let his hand rest for an instant upon the edge of the table between them, in the blue shadow of Mary's bowl of flowers. Estelle put out her own still-beautiful hand to adjust a strand of fern which was trailing low, and in withdrawing it again let her palm brush the back of his hand, and her finger-tips pass over his knuckles in a caress as subtle as it was audacious. The antique garnet ring on her middle finger was one he had given her sixteen years ago. He had an excellent memory; it was not necessary to steal a glance at his still profile to be sure that he had recognised his gift, and assessed its implications here.

Now she knew what she wanted. Her spirits rose buoyantly, she addressed her heart pleasurably to the fight.

Dr Benson came in for coffee after dinner, as he often did when his evenings remained undisturbed by patients; a small, grey, dry man with shrewd eyes and a patiently sceptical smile. He always made a point of calling casually, upon some friendly pretext or other, whenever Helen was about to make the journey to London for a broadcast; nothing was said about professional matters, he simply observed the evidences of her health and spirits and, if he was satisfied, proffered no advice. This devoted watchfulness seemed to Bill no more than Helen's due, but it was one more evidence of her beneficent power, and it always gave him pleasure.

Then the rector came in through the french windows from the garden, for he was an intimate of the household at Hugonin's Mill from some years back. A good-looking, middle-aged man with a face at once anxious and complacent, the double fruit, so Philip had once said, of an invalid wife and a fat living. Mrs Clive had made a previous marriage of disastrous memory with an artist by the beautiful name of Pharamond, and had never quite (said Philip again) been able to reconcile her relief at moving into the fold of sanctity with her secret nostalgia for the raffish society of her first match; so she had withdrawn from the insoluble problem into a yellow hypochondria. It wasn't often her daughter put in an appearance in the village these days. The rarity of her duty visits to the rectory indicated that she had voted firmly for Bohemia; for she was well on the way to becoming a sculptress at twenty-one, and Pharamond's daughter from head to foot. It was a surprise when she came in from the gathering darkness at her stepfather's shoulder, and half-closed her large dark eyes against the gay lights of the hall like a cat.

Rachel was the contradiction of everything Bill had ever admired or wanted in a woman. She entered the presence of acquaintances and strangers alike without a social smile, her clothes were not chosen to please anyone but herself, her young face with its spare flesh and resolute bones could have been a boy's face, and the hands with which she accepted her coffee-cup were strong and square, with short, untinted finger-nails, workman's hands. All the same, she had an assured physical distinction, her father's legacy, and a quality of uncompromising thoughtfulness which was not to be confused with consideration. She was capable of saying the wrong thing after deliberation, but she was never likely to do so without thinking.

'Canada!' she said inevitably, when she heard the location of Gerard Renaud's largest business interests. 'Bill here is thinking of going into some mining project in your country, Mr Renaud. Unless he's changed his plans since I was here last, that is.'

'He hasn't,' said Philip promptly, 'but it's high time he did. Mining with Peter Lawson is out – definitely, finally out, I'll see to that. Do you think you could induce him to realise it, Rachel? I'd be grateful – reiteration bores me.'

Bill was aware of a momentary congestion of slightly embarrassed glances taking stock of him, and of his own suffused face, and hated Philip for an instant with all his heart, and Rachel hardly less. He opened his mouth to make an angry rejoinder, and felt Helen's soft hand on his wrist, subduing him with a touch. She gave him a warning frown, and a quick, comforting smile, and deflected the battery of eyes back upon her husband.

'Philip can't bear having to talk or think about business in any shape or form. In any case, he's hardly fit for human company when he has proofs to correct. I'm surprised he's still with us,' she said, meeting her husband's eyes with a teasing smile. 'It can't be a social conscience, because he hasn't one; it must be Mrs Renaud's influence.'

'Work,' said Philip, 'is for the middle of the night, when no beguiling company offers. There's no other way of getting rid of proofs, in any case. I can sometimes write among distractions, but never, never correct proofs without being absolutely alone, and safe from anything that might deflect my attention. At that stage I always hate the thing so much that I'd make use of any pretext to leave it and forget it ever happened.'

They received this pronouncement with indulgent smiles, no one believing him; no one except, perhaps, Rachel, who stood looking at him sombrely, with lowered brows, and underlip protruding dubiously. Philip was not smiling, either; but then, Philip never smiled at his own jokes.

'Then why do you write them?' asked Rachel quite bluntly.

'It's expected of me. And they earn money. I doubt if I've got time to learn another trade now in time to make a living at it.'

'It must be awful,' said Rachel, 'to have to do work for which you haven't any respect.'

'Rachel!' protested the rector gently, and hurried to cover the sudden gulf of embarrassment she had opened under their feet. 'Every vocation seems to have these periods of losing its savour. Without reflection on the work one is actually doing at the time, too – it happens sometimes in a man's most fruitful period. What is performed with most difficulty and pain, and least satisfaction, is often one's best work in spite of its hard birth. But I should have thought in your line of country you might be immune – there's such an intrinsic interest in mystery stories, such a challenge in working out a problem. I very much enjoyed your last book.'

'Did you, Rector? How kind! I'd never thought of you as a reader of murder mysteries.'

'Murder?' said Gerard, suddenly raising his eyes from the garnet ring on his wife's hand to Philip's saturnine face. 'That's what you deal in, is it?'

It seemed a strange subject in which to take refuge from stresses which were beginning to set all their nerves on edge; and yet at the time it appeared so remote from them all that they could afford to be detached about it. Especially Philip, whose curious stock-in-trade it was. Among so many dangerous personal relationships, this surely provided ground on which they could meet in a discussion so academic that it need disturb none of them. Bill could dissemble the frustration of which he had just been roughly reminded, Estelle could recover from her momentary contortion of rage at the placidity with which Helen seemed to dismiss any possibility of rivalry between them, Gerard could memorise the antique outlines of the garnet ring he had never seen on his wife's hand until now, and ponder its origin silently, while they all talked about murder.

In the event it was Philip who did most of the talking.

'Murders are committed so easily on paper,' Gerard said sceptically, 'but in real life they seem to me to provide a lot of practical difficulties.'

'Do you think so? The difficulties often seem to me to be more apparent than real. Every man carries about with him the possibility of his own destruction; it's only necessary to know him well enough, to know the habits of his mind and the ruts of his routine, in order to kill him. Of course, if you haven't the patience to study the ground thoroughly you'll come to grief, but if you really take the trouble to know your subject he'll point out the chinks in his armour himself sooner or later. In every life there's some foible, or prejudice, or weakness, through which the careful finger of hate can penetrate. Men make their own deaths – even their own murders. Every man provides the occasion and the weapon, even if for most of us there happens to be no enemy at hand to make use of them.'

'You are relieving man of his responsibility for his acts,' protested the rector, bridling like a woman now that Philip had set a deliberate foot on his own professional territory.

'No,' said Rachel instantly, 'he's only pointing out that responsibility is never a single or a simple matter.'

'I'm not sure that I understand you,' said Gerard, looking up at Philip steadily through his thick lenses. 'Say, for instance, that *I* had some motive for wanting to murder *you* – how would I set about it, supposing I had the patience and the time to do it your way?'

'Very well, by all means take my own case. You'll hardly believe it, but, however difficult my temperament may be at other times, when I'm working I'm a creature of rigid habit, and my day's vulnerable at a dozen points, well-known to all the household and a large number of my friends outside it. It wouldn't take much observation to get the hang of my routine. For instance, when I'm working I retire to my glory-hole up there,' he said, indicating by a wave of his hand the door at the head of the staircase, where the little gallery made latticed shadows against the lofty roof of the hall, 'about ten o'clock, and work half the night, all night if my deadline is catching up with me. No inspiration is involved – I do it on coffee. Mary makes a large pot of it just before she goes to bed about eleven. She's a creature of habit, too, so it always is about eleven, and it's always the same old black ceramic pot with the flowers, that Helen bought me on our honeymoon, with a matching cup – we broke the second one long ago – and she always tiptoes up and puts it on the table outside my door, and tiptoes away again. Mary, bless her, is the one person in the world, apart from Helen, who has any reverence for my work. So she never gives me a knock, for fear of interrupting the muse, and as often as not I don't remember the tray until nearly midnight. It stands out there for anything

133

from ten minutes to three-quarters of an hour before I remember to fetch it in and drink it, and the whole household marches past it to bed, there being nothing to do here after about eleven, except go to bed. How easy, how very easy, instead of laying elaborate plots that are sure to leave a loose end somewhere, simply to wait for an occasion when the house has enough people in it to render your presence no more conspicuous than anyone else's, and drop something lethal into the coffee-pot! True, it would entail getting hold of the something lethal by strictly private means, and something not so volatile as to lose its potency during the half-hour interval – but it wouldn't really present much of a problem, because, you see, it needn't be something that left no trace. The traces would only end in mid-air, among half a dozen people who shared the same opportunity. Then all you would have to do would be keep your nerve, admit nothing, know nothing, do nothing. No, all you need to kill efficiently is patience, placidity and the ability to observe accurately. The rest the victim himself provides. Every murdered man, in fact,' said Philip, with his perverse, dark smile, 'is in some degree a suicide. As every suicide has, in a sense, been murdered.'

The meditative little lecture ended, and there was a brief silence of uncertainty and disapproval. Only Rachel, standing in the shadows by the window with her large and daunting eyes fixed upon Philip, shook back her black hair, and pursued with evident enjoyment:

'Would you extend that theory to the deaths of classes – nations – civilisations? Rome going down before Attila – was that a suicide, too? And aren't we always being told that our own highly moral civilisation is already doomed? What's the verdict going to be at that inquest?'

'Civilisations? They open the door to their own deaths, and sharpen the knives, and hand them to their heirs! As often as not they lean over and impale themselves. What I can't understand is how they manage to retain the capacity for surprise and indignation when they see the blood flow. Now *I*,' said Philip, reflecting Rachel's smile, 'shall not be in the least surprised, though I may retain enough human fallibility to feel slightly indignant.'

The rector exclaimed warmly: 'But really, Greville, I must protest! I know you're indulging a fantasy – a rather ill-judged one, if I may say so – but to confuse the simple issues of right and wrong in this irresponsible way is a very bad example to—'

Philip and Rachel broke into speech together, he placidly, she hotly, crying that nothing in human experience could be less simple than these. The rector did not argue about the nature of right and wrong, he stated them in flat terms, by the book, washing his hands decisively of other people's sins, though he admitted, without conviction, the existence of his own. The hostility between him and his stepdaughter was probably a matter of temperament in the first place, but plainly it had flourished in its growth for a long time. He opposed to her passion only an impenetrable indulgence.

'By what compass, then, my dear child, *do* you hope to pick your way between right and wrong, since you despise the rules drawn up by the wise out of their experience?' His smile was invulnerable, because whatever she said, he would not argue with her seriously, and he who never argues can never be refuted.

'By the only honest compass I, or anyone else, can have in this world; my own judgment and my own conscience.'

'Responsible to no one?' he said, smiling indulgently.

'Responsible to God,' said Rachel, speaking the name with an aplomb and certainty he would have thought it unbecoming to use even in a sermon, 'who gave me the tools, and presumably intended me to use them. But not to any other person, or group, or church, or nation. And if I mistake my way, I'll be damned with goodwill, rather than crawl into your kind of heaven by your kind of rulebook, half a woman and a sterilised model of a soul!'

This defiance had arisen, or so it had seemed at first, entirely out of the antipathy between these two incompatible people, and was really a part in a disputation which had begun somewhere several years back, when their personalities first clashed, rather than relating to this small, half-serious argument on the ethics of murder and suicide. And yet the dark girl, with her fierce, challenging smile, had turned away from her uncle, and was facing full into the room, making her declaration of faith – for though it was a rejection of established standards it was, Bill supposed, in its way a declaration of faith – towards the assembly in general. Unwillingly he felt the stimulation of her perversity, and recognised pleasure in it, until he identified at last the exact point against which she was balancing her lance. The sting of incredulous resentment made him wince. Fair, quiet and immune in the middle of enmities, Helen sat with her long, delicate hands in repose along the arms of her chair, and her tranquil smile pardoning them all for the excesses of speech and fancy she could not share. It was the way she looked at children; children did not feel insulted by it, and adults, if they shared Helen's own wisdom and humility, were grateful for it. But after all, thought Bill, with an attempt at forbearance, this arrogant girl was at the sore stage between child and adult, and might almost be forgiven for flinching at the recognition of another woman's superiority.

'I must apologise,' said the rector, wryly smiling, 'for my daughter's modern usage. They call it being outspoken. I'm told they grow out of it, in time.'

'Only to acquire our complacency, probably,' said Helen. 'I'm not sure that it's a fair exchange.' She smiled at Rachel without protest or disapproval, in every dispute apart, no one's ally but everyone's friend, calming, reconciling, forgiving, asserting her excellence by never asserting it. She looked round the circle of faces with a deprecating little grimace. 'I'm so sorry, I hate to go, and please don't let me disturb anyone else – but Dr Benson's looking at me! I'm supposed to get plenty of rest before the journey tomorrow. Will you forgive me if I go to bed now?'

The rector rose at once, with apologies for failing to notice the length of their stay, and profuse hopes that they had not tired her, but she pressed him gently back into his chair, and declined with firmness to let her departure break up the evening. Though she knows, thought Estelle, her eyes fixed on the slender, straight back as Helen ascended the staircase, that it will! She knows that they all – except that wild girl, of course – move and breathe and function in attendance on her will. She's too sure of herself! Am I negligible, that she confides her husband to me for a whole day without even a qualm? She despises all competition. Well, we'll see! But for that, Helen Greville, I don't think I'd have bothered to take him from you. But now I will. But for that, I don't seriously think, on consideration, that I should have wanted him. But now I do want him! And now I'll take him!

Helen passed by the door of Philip's study, touching the panels with her finger-tips as she went by, and disappeared into the corridor beyond.

Bill, marking the moment of her vanishing, experienced again the sudden coldness of loss which of late had frightened him so unreasonably whenever she left his sight. It was almost indistinguishable from despair, and he attributed it to his own immediate anxiety, thinking miserably: 'It won't be any use, Philip won't give in. Not even for her! He's made it plain enough. If only it didn't depend on him – if only it was Helen—!'

Helen rose early in the morning. There was no need, as Mary, who was always up by seven, pointed out very gently, but Helen said she could not sleep with the sun so brilliant and the spring so visibly awake in the garden. She filled in the time by running happily about the mill, doing innumerable little jobs which Mary would have preferred to do herself, and apologised disarmingly for her own activities.

'I know I'm a nuisance. Don't be angry!' Her hands were full of yellow and red tulips fresh from the glossy turf by the river. 'They're for Philip's work-room. Don't tell him, let him find them after I've gone. I love doing things for him, and I shan't see him all day. Let me play!'

Mary did not say that whatever Helen did would be

perfect in her eyes, but her smile and her acquiescence were heavy with adoration. 'Only don't tire yourself out. Remember you've got a big day ahead of you. You really ought to take things easy until Bill drives you to the station.'

'There's nearly two hours yet. I shan't be tired, I promise you I shan't. I feel entirely well today. And in good voice! You'll see!'

She went to lift down from its shelf in the cabinet the black glaze coffee-pot and the one remaining cup Philip had described the previous evening. It was Japanese work, not old, but good of its kind. The pot was decorated within and without with a spray of a flowering tree, the white petals immaculate against the matt black. The same spray coiled within the cup. She passed a finger-tip over the slightly raised flowers, smiling to herself at all the memories this cup held.

'And I don't believe he ever really liked it, Mary – not for itself, I mean. He only loved it because I gave it to him, and afterwards because of all the days and nights it had seen with us.' She laid ready the little tray for the night, touching every piece with the same gentle, glowing smile. 'I know that wasn't necessary. I only wanted to do it myself. And now I'm going to take him his letters. He'll still be asleep – he worked so late, my poor darling.'

Philip opened his eyes upon her face, and instantly smiled. He had a way of being awake in one motionless leap into full consciousness and intense intelligence. He reached up a long arm out of the bed, and drew her down to the pillow beside him, her cheek against his cheek.

'Don't desert me! Don't go! Or let me come with you.'

'Darling, if only we could! But the Renauds—'

'Damn the Renauds!' he said, but his sigh was resigned and quiet. He knew that he would do whatever she expected of him.

'But I'm not deserting you, I'll never desert you. This evening you'll be with me. We have a secret assignation at ten minutes past ten, before the news. Thousands of people will be watching, and none of them will know. You won't forget to meet me?'

He turned his head, and pressed his face into the hollow of her shoulder, kissing her with slow, thoughtful pleasure. The lids of his closed eyes were sunken and blue with weariness. She stroked them very lightly with the tip of one delicate forefinger.

'You won't forget? If you weren't with me I should know, and I couldn't sing.'

'I shall be with you. Don't you know it? As long as you need me, I shall always be with you.'

She smiled over his greying head, reflecting tenderly within her secret mind whose was the need, and whose the power to satisfy needs.

'And afterwards, you won't go and work all night, will you? You're so tired, you ought to get a good night's sleep.'

'Yes,' he said comfortably into her soft shoulder. 'Yes, afterwards I'll sleep. I can finish the proofs in another half-hour, and then I promise you I'll sleep.'

They all came out on to the sweep of gravel before the mill to see her off. At the last moment she turned back from the open door of the car to kiss Philip again, lifting her face to him with a sudden impulsive passion. Estelle, watching from the doorstep, thought: 'Everything about her has to have the symbolic quality of a religious rite. And she's only leaving him until tomorrow! Saints are the very devil!' But the momentary stab of mingled amusement and animosity dissolved suddenly into the enchanting thought: 'Perhaps she's given herself away a little – perhaps she isn't as absolutely sure of herself as she likes to believe.' She thought of the long hours of the day and the night unrolling before her at leisure, and smiled to herself, turning the garnet ring upon her finger.

Bill drove the big car out from the gates and down the lane in expectant silence, waiting for Helen to say something about the commission he had entrusted to her; but when he reached the high-road, and halted dutifully at the line, and still she was silent, he could bear it no longer.

'Well, did you speak to him?' Helen looked round at him with a blank, blue stare of bewilderment, as though he had said something in a foreign language. 'About me!' he said, hurt and exasperated that she should allow so urgent a matter to slip out of her mind. 'What did he say? Did he listen to you?'

'I haven't talked to him about it yet, Bill. There's been no opportunity.' She had wrenched her mind to his concerns only with an effort, he could see that, but her voice now was mild and firm as ever, demanding of him more patience than he possessed.

He sent the car forward with a furious jerk. 'You forgot all about it!' he said, cut to the heart.

'If that's what you believe, my dear, then there's nothing I can say, is there?' Her soft voice held no note of reproach, but it flooded him with affectionate, unbearable memories of past goodness, and he drove for a few minutes struggling with his own temper and his instinctive and over-violent regrets. Quarrels with Uncle Philip had come and gone in his experience too often and too simply to be remembered long, or leave any scars; but a word amiss between him and Helen, and he was tormented with a fierce and immoderate remorse. His childhood had been overcharged with these extremities of feeling. He had never understood them; he was so much afraid of them that he had never tried looking at them very closely.

He stole a quick, shamefaced glance at Helen now, and his heart melted in his breast with frantic tenderness. She was gazing straight before her into air, her eyes wide and brilliant with tears. The car lurched as he reached over and shut a large palm over the slender hands clasped in her lap.

'Darling, forgive me! I didn't mean it! As though you'd ever let me down! As though I didn't know – Oh, God, I am a heel, to turn on *you*, just because *he's* made up his mind—'

Helen's soft mouth quivered into a startled smile. 'Do keep your mind on the road, Bill, you'll have us in the ditch. It's all right, don't worry. I know you were just letting off steam. But I didn't forget, and I shan't forget. Yes, I know I shall be away until tomorrow, and I know that leaves you only three days, but still you must trust me.'

'But it couldn't be done in three days, all the legal business, and everything. And Lawson won't wait any longer, he can't, he has to think of his own future—'

'Listen to me, Bill! You must have patience, you must

believe that I know best. I promise you I'm doing my best for you. I promise you that if this venture is really so important to you, you shall have what you want. Now are you satisfied?'

Of her affection and good faith he was indeed satisfied, but he could not feel equally assured of fate's good intentions towards him. A day lost was a day lost, and could never be recovered; Philip was fixed in his determination and when it came to the point Bill could not imagine him being shaken even by Helen's appeals. Ordinarily he would do whatever she wanted, but in this matter there was another person's wish to be considered; Philip was right, in a way, Bill conceded grudgingly, to adhere to what he believed his sister would have wanted him to do. If only it had rested with Helen, he was thinking again wretchedly, as he stopped the car in the station yard.

'I'll come and meet you tomorrow, off the ten o'clock train. Do take care of yourself.'

'You'll see me tonight,' she reminded him, smiling.

'Yes, of course! I wouldn't miss it!' He kissed her, the identical quick, dutiful kiss of all young men seeing their mothers off by train. At least, he had always supposed it to be the same model, making allowances for the extra tenderness he had felt towards Helen because she had really none of a mother's obligations towards him, and had cared for him rather out of the goodness of her quite superhumanly good heart. The pain and the pleasure that found their way into that brief contact of lips had always somewhat confounded him. But then, all the wounds and delights of life had seemed to him to be more extreme than other people admitted, and he had very early learned to dissemble them, too, in order to be exactly as other boys were.

Now, as he watched Helen's train move out, honesty compelled him to notice the discomfort of his own heart. He turned back to the car thinking incessantly, tormentedly, helplessly: 'I've got to get the money! I've got to get away!'

Gerard was standing beside the dressing-table, with the garnet ring in the palm of his hand, when his wife came in from the bathroom to dress for the evening. She looked from the little circle of gold to his face, which was as still and unrevealing as stagnant water. She was not disturbed. She could not conceive of any reaction of his moving her to any emotion beyond boredom, and she was not by nature a timorous woman. She was even a little cramped within her respectability, after a whole day of moving softly, pleasurably, nearer and nearer to a new footing with Philip, and would almost welcome, she thought, the stimulus of a fight, and the openness of behaving exactly as she chose again. She felt as though the thaw had set in in her bones, after seven years of frost.

'Do you like it?'

'It has a curious effect on me. It makes me clairvoyant. I ask myself, since when did my wife develop a taste for garnets and such small fry? Or is this, perhaps, a survival from the days when even garnets were not to be despised? There was a time, of course, when there were no diamonds to be had.' His voice was quite flat and low, and it was with astonishment that she saw the large, pale hand shaking as it held the ring.

'How like you,' she said agreeably, 'to remind me in

every crisis, however small, of your beastly money. It's true I enjoy it. It's also true I could live without it. I know more than one way of enjoying life.'

'So I observed,' said Gerard, 'just now when you took his hand beneath the tea-table. Beware of mirrors, Estelle!'

She had never seen him so still, or so precariously under control. Who would have thought there was any passion to be found in the inert mass? She let fall the thin nylon wrap from her shoulders and stretched up her arms, spreading out the skirt of the red-gold dress above her head. It was the exact colour of her hair, and had a comparable glitter about it.

'He gave you this ring,' said Gerard. It was not a question, and she made no answer. 'When?'

'Long before I ever knew you,' she said calmly, emerging radiant and indifferent from the golden tissue. 'And I hadn't set eyes on him since until the evening we met them in the theatre. What I did and didn't do before I met you can hardly affect you, can it?'

'I am not concerned with what you did before we met. I've never asked you any questions about what may have happened before. But I am concerned with what you do now. If the ring belongs to the past, why have you resurrected it now?'

'Why shouldn't I? It belongs to me, if I choose to wear it what is there to stop me?'

'For seven years you've never given it a thought, or I should have seen it before. Now suddenly you put it on, and spread out your hand before his eyes, for him to see that his gift still means something to you. And was that to be all, Estelle?'

'I never knew you had so much imagination,' she said, sitting down before the dressing-table within reach of his hand if he had chosen to touch her. 'A ring is something to be worn when one fancies it. So is a dress.'

'And a lover? And a husband? When one fancies them?'

'Since I married you,' she said, with a sudden fiery glare upward into his heavy face, 'I've been faithful to you.' And as soon as she had uttered the words she saw how astonishing they were, and cast about within herself almost disbelievingly for a reason. 'What more do you want?'

'Nothing more. Just as long as I have that. But be careful, Estelle, how you break bargains with me, even unspoken ones.' ·

It was not fear she felt, but this was a Gerard so strange to her that she did experience a chill of caution. She turned to face him, staring indignantly into his eyes, and her own were wide and clear.

'What do you think I've been doing? You've been within sight of me all day long – what have I done to make you so damned suspicious?'

'Do you really want me to tell you? You meet this man again after all these years, you – yes, now I think back to that evening, I see that you forced this invitation out of his wife. You fish out his ring from some corner where it's lain forgotten, and stick it on your finger, and insinuate your hand into his. And you ask me what reason I have to be suspicious! Well, fortunately for him – and for you, too! – he's out of your reach. He's in love with his wife! – that's something you wouldn't understand. Do you think she doesn't know what you're about? Do you think she wasn't sitting there, last night, enjoying the spectacle of you breaking your head against a rock?'

Estelle's hands clenched into fists in the coils of her shining hair, and the crystal comb snapped in two, and fell silently on to Helen's guest-room carpet. 'Damn you!' she said, in a muted scream of fury. 'Damn you, shut up!'

She loathed herself for it the next moment. How could she have been such a fool as to let him prise that betraying reaction out of her? She began to hate him then; the only amazing thing was that until that moment he had seemed far too dull to be worth hating.

He laughed, and it was a chilly and chilling sound. 'All the same, you should be glad of failure, my dear Estelle – let me advise you seriously, beware of success! It wouldn't be at all healthy – for you or for him!'

The door closed quietly upon his departure. Estelle sat staring into the mirror until he had vanished from its silver frame, and only the gracious room and her own beauty were left confronting her. And in a moment or two she had regained her shaken equilibrium, and the confidence he had so nearly drained out of her rose like a triumphant tide. She knew her Philip, all her adroitness in manipulating him was coming back to her. She knew herself and her capabilities. As for her husband's last threat, it was the kind of utterance that could have come only from a man who felt himself to be impotent; she dismissed it with a contemptuous smile, and began to make up her face.

Philip closed the door of his study and stretched out a hand towards the light-switch, and another hand came out of the deep dusk in the corner of the room and took him by the wrist, arresting the movement. He stiffened for an instant only, and then quite softly and delightedly he began to laugh. And he did not switch on the light.

'My dear Estelle! My dear girl! How like you! May I put on the desk-light, at least? It would be nice to see you – that was always a pleasure, and believe me, it still is. The curtains are already drawn, I see – that was thoughtful of you.'

'I am thoughtful – had you forgotten? How lucky that you're not one of those authors who lock the doors of their work-rooms.' She herself reached out and switched on the reading-light on the desk; the confined shadows it cast did not reach the curtains at the window.

'And how is your headache now? Better, I trust?' His voice, even in mockery, was perforce an intimate whisper. In the hall below the others were talking steadily, the murmur of their conversation came up as though from a great distance.

'So much better that I shall be able to come down and enjoy Helen's recital, in half an hour or so – if Helen's husband sees fit to complete the cure!' She drew near to him very softly, her eyes shining with laughter. He made no move to meet her or to retreat from her, but stood quite still as she slid her hands upward to his shoulders, and her warmth and her faint, sweet scent touched him together. 'How long have we? How long ought it to take you to find one of your own novels on your own shelves?'

'How did you know Mary wouldn't simply come in here and fetch it herself, and bring it straight to you?'

'Mary touch anything in your holy of holies? Never! No, I knew she'd have to send you up to get it yourself.

Are you angry?' A question no one ever asks in that particular tone without first knowing the answer.

'Oh, my sweet, crazy, darling girl, angry? I can't thank you enough! Here was I thinking old age already had me by the tail, and all the bloom was off me for good, and you blaze into the house like a comet and get me feeling young again! It's a compliment I won't forget to you.'

Her hands stole round his neck, and drew him against her breast; and in a moment she felt his arms go gently round her. 'Philip! You must have seen, you must have known, how I still feel about you. We made the worst mistake of our lives when we separated. I've been miserable ever since, and you – you can't go on for the rest of your life living on milk and water! That's no diet for you!'

He was quivering gently in her embrace, and at first she thought that it was with passion, but when he spoke there was no mistaking the deep tremors of laughter, a teasing, affectionate laughter that made her heart sink.

'I think maybe a milk diet's all I can digest these days, Estelle, my love. And as for you, there's many a woman would be glad to be miserable with you, if it would give her your blooming looks. I like to think of you lying awake all night regretting the old days, but it doesn't come easy. It's no use, my dear, it's too late to reform me – I'm a married man clean through to the heart, and all the devilry's gone out of me. What use would I be to you, and me fifteen years on a lowering diet?'

'Philip the married man!' she whispered, with her lips against his cheek and her fingers in his hair. 'I can't believe you've really changed so much. How could you be satisfied with this? Have you been happy? Can you truthfully tell me you've been happy?'

'I've had what I wanted most in the world – if that's the same thing.'

'It isn't! Addicts want drugs more than anything in the world, but they die of them in the end. I could make you come alive again.'

'You could make stones get up and walk,' he said, smiling. 'But I'm not a stone, I'm a poor, helpless married man who's lost his taste for adventures, and is past praying for.'

Caressing him with hands, and arms, and lips, in a frenzy of disbelief, she whispered in a trembling voice: 'I love you, Philip, I love you—'

'And I love you, devilment and all, but I doubt if we mean the same thing. I'm not what I was, and you're to the last letter what you've always been, and there's no going back. And what's more, you don't really want it any more than I do. And now go on back to the headache you left in your room, because I'm going down to hand over your book to Mary, and in five minutes she'll be up to bring it in to you.' He enveloped her suddenly in a hearty hug and, taking her by the chin, kissed her emphatically, without reluctance, even with unmistakable enjoyment, but with the large, unembarrassed calm of a man quite at peace with his present and his past. It was the quality of that calm that turned her blood to gall within her, and the kiss to acid on her mouth. She was so stunned that when he released her and turned cheerfully away she let him get to the door before she could find strength to move. Then she sprang silently after him, and wrenched him round by the shoulder to face her again.

'Philip, is that all you have to say to me? Do you know what you're doing?'

He frowned, touching a finger warningly to her lips. 'Keep your voice down! And wait until I've gone half-way down the stairs before you slip back to your room – even when the landing light's off they can see this door vaguely from below. Of course I know what I'm doing! I'm going down to give Mary the novel you felt you'd like to read – and you'd better be there to receive it when she brings it up to you. And then I'm going to make rea-sonably civilised conversation with your husband until it's time to turn on the TV for my wife's recital – which is what I'm really waiting for.' He touched Estelle's pale and rigid cheek with a sympathetic finger. The soft thread of a voice said wryly: 'Oh, my dear, we're not children any more. We grew up an uncomfortably long time ago. And in an uncomfortably short time now we're going to grow old. I'm not forgetting anything, believe me, or regretting anything, either. But I'm not such a fool as to think I can live my green days all over again.'

The spot where his touch had rested burned her. She put up a cold hand to rub the mark away. 'And I mean nothing to you!'

'You mean very much, high spirits, fun, fine memories, beauty, kindness.'

'But not love! *She* means that to you!'

'Since you understand only one thing by that word – yes, Helen means that to me.'

He smiled at her, and he was gone. She stood where he had left her, cold now to the heart with humiliation and rage. She thought that if she could have killed him at that moment she would have done it, and felt healed and vindicated in the act.

'Helen Greville ends this Good Friday recital with two arias by Bach. First, she sings *"Komm, süsser Tod"* – "Come, sweet death"—'

Unbelievably fair and delicate, Helen stood in her austere white dress in the semi-circle of strings, and sang. Her pure minor talent was ideally suited to the television screen; she came fresh to the medium, and had not yet acquired the technique of restlessness; she simply stood and sang, her hands lightly clasped under her breast. And the cameras were subdued by her stillness and the solemnity of the occasion to a quite unusual repose, moving with subtlety and tenderness over her beauty. For in song she kept her beauty unimpaired. She sang smiling, and when she was deeply moved, as now, the smile had a kind of anguish in it.

'Come, sweet death, come, desired rest—' sang Helen, clearly and solemnly against the organ's deep, sombre tone.

In the darkened room, which only she illuminated, Philip sat with his chin on his hand, his eyes fixed upon the miniature Helen in the screen. Not two yards away from him, rigid in her chair, and as intent upon his profile as he upon his wife's radiant whiteness, Estelle sat burning in her own rage and grief, and somewhere in the darkness beyond her Gerard watched her as narrowly. He had not believed for a moment in her headache; she never had headaches. And yet she was certainly ill, her sick pallor proclaimed it; she was ill with a disease rest and aspirins and a darkened room wouldn't cure.

'And finally, from Cantata Number one hundred and fifty-nine, "*Es ist vollbracht*" – "It is finished—" '

The oboe *obbligato*, inexpressibly sad and pure and final, played round Helen's stillness like an air from heaven, sourceless and miraculous. Her clear voice lifted quietly after it, uttering the last ecstasy of achievement and despair. '*Es ist vollbracht, es ist vollbracht—*' soaring first to resolution and triumph, sinking afterwards to the composure of death, and absolution from all further effort and all further hope or pain. She looked out from the screen suddenly in close-up, full-face, her singing, smiling mouth convulsed with grief, and tears swimming in her eyes. She looked into her husband's rapt and quiet face until the aria ended, and it was as though they were alone together, somewhere far from the world. And then the announcer was closing the programme with suitable reverence, and the shock of change made them all start and shiver as the preliminary shot for the news appeared in the screen.

Philip jumped out of his chair with a movement of violent suddenness, and switched off. There was an instant of complete darkness in the room. Somewhere close to the french window, which stood open upon the sleeping garden, a voice repeated softly: 'The end is come – the pain is over—'

Bill, startled, reached up and fumbled for the light-switch, and in the abrupt blaze Rachel stood wide-eyed in the frame of the window, staring at him wildly for an instant, as people do after darkness, and having about her, as suddenly appearing out of air, something at once dazzling and sinister, an over-significance, a symbolic virtue. Her lips were still curved upon the free translation of the wonderful and terrible words of the Bach aria, words which belonged to the last ebb of the hope of man, before anyone dreamed of resurrection. The moment of the victory of evil, to all appearances permanent, final, beyond appeal. Bill saw all this in Rachel's brooding face, and it was terrifying; and it had always been there for the imaginative to see for themselves, yet until now he had never seen it. It made light, and movement, and gaiety, and good faith, suddenly a thousand times more wonderful, to have experienced that moment and survived it to remember Easter Day, which was as surely coming.

'Did I startle you?' said Rachel, moving forward into the light. 'I'm sorry! I came in almost at the beginning, but I didn't care to disturb you all. I knew Mr Greville wouldn't mind if I walked in.'

Philip said: 'Of course not!' but he said it like a sleep-walker, his eyes still turned inward upon the remembered vision of his wife. 'I'm glad you looked in.'

'I mustn't stay. I just wanted to hear and see Helen.'

'And she was magnificent!' said Gerard, stirring heavily in his chair, and watching every tremor of his wife's haggard face.

'Oh, Helen's an artist, all right,' said Rachel simply. From her there could scarcely be higher praise, and she said it with conviction.

Mary offered drinks, and they sat for an uneasy while making desultory conversation round their host, who sat silent and absent from them still, and presently rose with a murmured apology, and said good night. They watched him climb the stairs and vanish into his study, closing the door behind him with a finality no one was likely to challenge. With Helen's going the evening had ended. Unless, perhaps, for Bill at least, there had been one last significant moment, Rachel's entry in the dazzling darkness and light of revelation; and even that had all been part of Helen's spell. Nor could anything of importance happen now until Helen's return; they might as well go to bed, they were only sitting in an uncomfortable vacuum between a day which had already ended, and one which could not yet begin.

They all felt it. Rachel stayed only long enough to take the edge of abruptness from her coming and going, and then said good night. It was dark outside; Bill supposed, rather grudgingly, that he ought to walk home with her to the rectory, and made the offer with only a lukewarm grace, but she accepted it at once. Mary rolled up her knitting and went to make Philip's coffee, and was presently seen mounting the stairs with the little black ceramic tray, and laying it on the table outside his door. She hesitated, wondering if she ought not to come down and pick up the hospitable duties Philip had kicked out of his way with so little ceremony, keeping his guests company until they chose to go to bed; but Gerard looked up from the hall and met her eyes with a masterful stare, and said with emphasis: 'Good night, Miss Greville!' And after all, Bill would be back from the rectory soon, she thought, not displeased with this dismissal. They might like to sit talking for some time yet.

'Good night! Good night, Mrs Renaud, I do hope you'll have a good sleep, and feel better in the morning.'

'Thank you!' said Estelle mechanically. 'I'm sure I shall. Good night!'

Mary's steps receded along the long corridor. They

were alone in the hall. On the landing the door of Philip's room remained closed, and from behind it they caught now, in the stillness, faint strains of music, a clear, high voice from an infinite distance.

'Records of Helen,' said Gerard, with a vengeful smile. 'Do you hear? He can never have enough of her.'

He crossed the hearth and stood over his wife, who sat staring up at him with a bleak and open hostility he had never seen in her face before. 'Estelle, I don't ask what has passed between you and him. Oh, for God's sake don't try to deny that there's been anything. Do you think I'm stone blind? I only say, let it end here – let it end now! Don't push me any further, and I'll forget this ever happened. But if you persist in humiliating yourself and me—'

Was her failure to be read as clearly as that in her face? Her stunned pride rose flaming into life again; she glared up at her husband, and forced her rigid countenance to do the impossible. She looked him full in the eyes, and laughed.

'Are you so very sure of yourself, Gerard? Do you really think I'm as incompetent as all that? Don't you think he was rather a long time finding that book for me tonight? Does it take as long as that to say no, do you suppose?'

His heavy face hung over her still smiling with vengeful disbelief, and yet already mottled purple with doubt and fear and fury. 'You were there in the room with him! No! I don't believe it – it's impossible!'

'He was wiping my lipstick from his lips,' she said, laughing softly, 'as he came down the stairs. Didn't you notice? I thought you noticed everything! Yes, I was with

156

AUNT HELEN

him, there in the room! We made good use of the time –
do you want me to go into details?'

'I don't believe it!' he said, panting. 'He can't even see
anyone but her – he has no use for you – I saw it in your
face when you came down—'

'Can you see it there now?' And she turned her beautiful, laughing, flushed face to the light, and her violet
eyes glittered like amethysts with feverish triumph. 'Oh,
we can both act a little when it seems expedient! Only I'm
sick of expediency, it's no longer worth the effort – not
for all your money, my dear! Yes, I was with him! Yes,
I'll go to him again, whenever I please! Are you satisfied
now?'

She sprang out of her chair, and pushed her way past
him towards the staircase, feeling her enforced
complacency beginning to shatter in rage and pain. He
caught her by the arm, blindly, blunderingly, as she
passed by, and swung her round to face him. With astonishment and contempt she saw tears in his eyes.

'I won't let you do this! I'll kill you first, and him, too!
You're my wife! If you betray me, I'll kill you! Let him
alone! From now on, let him alone, I warn you – I warn
you!' His voice was thick and broken, as though he had
suffered a stroke.

She knew it was time to be a little afraid, but she
was so full of bitterness that there was no room for
fear. She wrenched herself free, and flung away from
him.

'I'll do as I please! You mean nothing to me – do
you hear? – nothing! I'm sick and tired of pretending
you do.'

She ran up the stairs, and he saw her hesitate for a long

157

moment outside the closed door of Philip's room. Then she ran on, and vanished into the corridor beyond.

Gerard slumped down with his misery into the chair she had vacated, and sat motionless for a long time. When he did move, it was only to pour himself a stiff drink, and swallow it quickly, and follow it up with another. The level in the decanter went down rapidly. If he could not drown his grief perhaps he could deaden it a little, in time. When he heard Bill's footsteps on the flags outside the french window, he dragged himself hurriedly to his feet, and stumbled clumsily but quietly up the stairs.

Bill, coming in from the garden, found the room empty, and there was nothing for him to do but lock up, put out the lights, and follow the rest of the household to bed. He made his rounds dutifully, but at the last moment he stood for a long time in miserable indecision outside Philip's door. Should he go in? Should he make one more attempt to talk to his uncle? Could he keep his temper this time? And would it do any good, even if he did?

Softly and clearly within the room rose the voice of Helen, singing again, on a record now three years old: '*Es ist vollbracht.*' 'The end is come – the pain is over—'

'What's the good!' thought Bill, wretchedly. 'If I go in there and interrupt him now he'll only throw me out with a flea in my ear. No, it's no use – not that way, at any rate!' He looked down moodily at the coffee tray, and his hand cupped the rounded breast of the pot for a moment before he passed reluctantly on towards his own room, putting out the landing light after him.

It was perhaps ten minutes later when Philip opened his door, and took in the tray.

'Philip hasn't come down yet,' said Mary, coming in from the kitchen-garden as Bill was finishing a very late breakfast. 'I wonder if I ought to wake him?'

'I shouldn't. I expect he's been up half the night, working. Helen always leaves him to sleep it out. Aren't the Renauds down yet, either?'

'He is – he finished breakfast long before you put in an appearance – not that he ate much, I must say – and he went out for a walk. I expect he didn't want to disturb his wife yet. But Philip will be annoyed if I let him sleep on, and he isn't up to welcome Helen home when she comes.'

'Well, if you wake him about the time I start for the station, that'll give him time to be up and waiting for her when we get back.'

It happened, therefore, that Mary, carrying a cup of tea, entered Philip's bedroom perhaps thirty seconds before Bill took the key of the garage from its hook in the kitchen, and walked out to fetch the car. So he was still just within earshot when the cup shattered on the edge of the bedside table, and the small, hoarse, unbelieving cry quavered out after the crash, not a loud cry, but so out of place in this sunny morning as to be inexpressibly shocking. His foot was on the doorstep when he heard it; he jumped round in haste, and ran back through the hall.

Mary came across the landing in a stiff, dazed, hurrying walk, her hand at her mouth, her eyes blank with horror. She looked through her nephew, as he came bounding up towards her, and gave no sign of seeing him, until he took her by the shoulders abruptly, and shook her.

'What's wrong? Aunt Mary, what is it? What happened?'

The alarm and concern in his voice seemed to reach her. She started in his arms, and blinked dazedly into his face. She began to shake between his hands as he held her.

'Bill, something's happened to Philip! He won't wake up! I touched him – he's cold – Bill, I think he's dead!'

Chapter 2

Bill knelt down by Philip's bed, and held the mirror from the dressing-table to the half-open lips, but it remained clear of any hopeful trace of mist. He touched the grey forehead, smoothed now of the troubling lines of thought, and drew back his fingers with a shiver from the coldness of the skin. Philip lay on his back, his face uplifted to the morning light, his arms relaxed and easy in the folds of the sheets. He looked young, and aloof, and ironical, wearing still the half-smile with which he had fallen asleep.

'Is he dead?' Mary asked in a whisper. But she knew, she had known from the first moment. Never could Philip have looked like that alive, whether waking or asleep.

Bill said: 'Yes.' The word was almost inaudible, as though shock had done something to his vocal cords. He cleared his throat laboriously, and slowly stood up. In the act he accomplished several stages of the transition into manhood, though all he understood of it was that the weight of events had suddenly come down upon his shoulders, and that instinctively he braced himself to receive the load. There was no time to avoid it, no opportunity to deflect it on to somebody else. There was nobody else, except Mary, and she was hovering at his back, still half-stunned with shock, and surprisingly helpless when confronted with the unforeseen, she whose daily routine ran on well-regulated tracks, like a train.

'But it isn't possible! How could he die? Why should he? There was nothing the matter with him. His heart was sound as a bell. People don't just die in the night for no reason—'

'I don't know, Aunt Mary, I don't know any more than you do. We shall have to call Dr Benson.' He had to make an intense effort to remember the steps which had to be taken after a sudden death, but this at least was certain, and urgent. The doctor who had been in attendance in the household must be called in at once, and he would give a death certificate. Or, of course, refuse one! There might have to be an inquest! Indeed, now that he had thought of that possibility, he saw that it was very likely in these circumstances. But only Dr Benson could decide. He took Mary by the arm, very gently, and led her out of the room and into Philip's study next door, and put her into a chair. The stunned and motionless look was still on her face, and her hands, when he took them in his, were stiff and cold.

'Darling, I'm going to get you a drink, whether you like the stuff or not. Don't try to think, or move, or do anything yet – you've had a bad shock. Just sit here till I come back, I'll see to everything.'

Perhaps it was the wrong treatment. Perhaps he was taking away from Mary, by thus assuming responsibility, the very thing she most needed, the necessity of coping with events. But she looked so helpless and witless that he couldn't spare time to rouse her yet, he would have to get on with it himself. There was the doctor, first of all – and what followed would depend on him. And there was Helen's train, drawing steadily nearer to the station, and no one to meet her. He couldn't possibly leave here now. Renaud might quite well be asked to meet the train, but Renaud was out walking somewhere, and Bill didn't know where, and hadn't time to hunt for him. Perhaps the rector would go. Helen – Helen—At the thought of her his emotions, which had been in a state of suspended animation since the terrible thing happened, started into vehement and painful life again. Poor Helen, he thought wildly, poor Philip, the two figures moving in and out in a tragic dance in his mind. He couldn't bear the thought of the rector breaking the news to her. But who else was there? And it was unthinkable that she should be left unmet, wondering what had happened, driving in anxiously by taxi to find her husband dead and her household in chaos.

Dr Benson answered the telephone from his surgery. Bill poured out the naked facts without finesse; there was no time for softening blows, especially for the benefit of this tough old professional, even if he had known Philip for fifteen years and been in a very real measure his friend.

'Can you come over as soon as possible? Don't leave anyone who really needs you, because there isn't anything you can do for Uncle Philip – but do come as soon as you can. He's dead! He didn't come down this morning, and Aunt Mary went up to wake him, and found him dead in bed. He looks as if he was quite fast asleep when he died, and never knew anything about it. No, we haven't touched anything. No, there's no doubt at all. He's cold—!' Bill heard his own voice split in two, and gulped down determinedly the constriction in his throat. 'Mary might need a sedative – she's badly shaken. I'm going to dope her with brandy.'

'Don't overdo it,' said Dr Benson briefly. 'I'll be there inside ten minutes.'

Bill pushed down the receiver rest for a moment, and dialled the rectory number. He still didn't like the idea, but he had no choice; and Helen, after all, in her charitable innocence, had the best of opinions of the rector, without any of the slight reservations the rest of the household felt about him. Tact without warmth seemed to Bill an offence, but it might have its uses. He braced himself to meet the inevitable condolences as gracefully as he could.

But it was not the rector who answered, it was Rachel Pharamond. Bill had never expected to feel such relief at the sound of that fresh, incisive young voice.

'Oh, Rachel, thank God it's you! Will you do us a great favour? It's frightfully urgent. I was to have met Helen's train at ten, and now something ghastly has happened, and I can't leave here, and she mustn't, simply mustn't, be left to come home alone and find out what's happened without any warning. It's Philip – we found him dead in bed, ten minutes ago. The doctor's on his way over now.'

'Wait a minute – it must be the line – I thought you said *Philip* was *dead*—!'

'He is! Aunt Mary found him. He must have died in his sleep. I know—! We can't believe in it, either. But there isn't any doubt about it.'

'Philip!' said Rachel, on a great, exhaled breath. 'Oh,

God, Bill, I'm so sorry! I liked him so much! Yes, I'll go for Helen, of course! There's time – I'll be there before the train gets in, don't worry.'

How prompt she was in decisions, and how blessedly brief in giving voice to sympathy! She almost rang off before he could call her back in sudden agitation: 'Rachel – don't tell her he's dead! Please! If you could just prepare her a little – say I rang up and asked you to come – say there's something wrong, and I couldn't come myself, but don't – I'd rather—'

'That's all right,' said Rachel. 'You shall break the news to her yourself. I'm just a stand-in for the journey. Good-bye, Bill!'

She was gone. He was amazed at the feeling of gratitude he had for her directness, and the absolute reliance he found himself placing in her. He went back at once to Mary, and coaxed and compelled her into swallowing the brandy he had brought for her. It quickened colour in her cheeks again, and made her shudder and grimace, which at least was better than that blank, fixed look of shock. She began to look round uneasily, convinced that in this or any crisis she ought to be hard at work, doing with competence whatever had to be done.

'Dr Benson's on his way. There's nothing we can do until he comes, except perhaps tell the Renauds what's happened.'

'And there's poor Helen just coming home – Oh dear, we'd forgotten her! How can we tell her? They adored each other so! And there's nobody to meet her, even!' Mary's tears brimmed over, and whether they were for Helen or for Philip was something Bill could not guess. He put his arm round her shoulders rallyingly, and hugged her for a moment, applying a technique of comfort which had gone out with his childhood, but might have its uses yet.

'It's all right, Aunt Mary, there'll be somebody to meet her. Rachel is going. I just telephoned her. Won't you go down now, and take care of Mrs Renaud, if she's put in an appearance? Things have got to go on, you know, for Helen's sake – for all our sakes. I'll stay here with Uncle Philip till the doctor comes.'

'Poor Bill,' said Mary, wiping her eyes, 'it's just as awful for you. It's as if the ground had opened under the house. He was so very *alive*!'

She rose, however, with some of her old briskness, and looking round with eyes still slightly dazed, observed the evidences of her brother's last preoccupations. On his desk the unfinished proof was pushed aside to make room for a pile of gramophone records, and the player still stood open on its cabinet. Beside the records, on a corner of the desk, lay the coffee tray, the bottom of the single cup dark with grounds.

'I may as well take that down, I suppose,' she said sadly, and stretched out her hands to pick it up. Bill checked her with a hand on her arm, hardly yet realising himself the significance of what he did.

'No, leave it. We ought not to touch anything yet. We don't know—'

He stopped, his eyes suddenly fixed in appalled remembrance on the black ceramic pot. He heard Philip's thoughtful, dispassionate voice lecturing on the psychology of successful murder, saying with deliberation: 'All you need to kill efficiently is patience, placidity, and the ability to observe accurately.' Bill felt sick,

166

and recognised with humiliation that he was horribly frightened. This death was altogether too apt. Had there been among Philip's audience one pupil willing to learn the technique literally? Somebody – was it Renaud? – had put the exact case as an instance. 'Say *I* wanted to murder *you* – how would I set about it?' And Philip had told them, in so many words, leaning forward to impale himself on the knife he himself had sharpened and handed to his murderer. Every victim of murder, he had said, is to some extent a suicide.

It isn't true, Bill told himself frantically, shaking the nightmare remembrance away from him. There'll be something quite prosaic, something we ought to have known about, something he should have been worrying about, an enlarged heart, an aneurism, something natural. The doctor will know. It's just one effect of shock, this running to invent trouble. Snap out of it. There was coffee in the pot, and that was all!

It was at that moment that they heard Dr Benson's feet stumping up the stairs. He would have left his car by the farm-gate, as usual, and come across the field and the bridge into the garden, letting himself in unannounced, as he always did. He had been in and out of the house so often in attendance on Helen that no ceremony ever attached to his visits. Mary hurried to meet him on the landing, and he gave her merely an abstracted pat on the shoulder and a jerk of his head backward down the stairs.

'One of your guests just came in from the lane, Mary. I'd go and keep him occupied for a while, if I were you. This is a bad business, we'd better know a bit more about it before we make it public property.'

She went down at once, grateful to have something definite to do again, now that she had so far recovered herself as to feel the want of action. Bill led the doctor into Philip's room, and stood back, watching with strained attention, as he made his rapid and careful examination. Neither of them said a word throughout this process. Bill fixed his eyes upon Philip's leaden face, with its ironical half-smile already smoothing out into a grand and humbling indifference, and waited with a thumping heart for the verdict. At length the doctor drew up the sheet over the dead man's face, and turned and looked at Bill for a long moment in silence.

'Well?' said Bill in a hoarse whisper, when he could no longer bear the waiting.

'It isn't well, Bill, my boy! It's far from well! I went over Philip about six months ago, when he'd been over-doing it badly, and I know he was fundamentally sound – heart, lungs, everything. Just run-down from over-work, but at bottom as strong as an ox. Healthy people like Philip don't go out overnight, like this. I'm sorry, Bill, but I can't give a certificate. I'm really very sorry, but where a death doesn't make sense it's my duty to pass on the job to the coroner. You understand what that means?'

'Yes,' said Bill with difficulty. 'It means an inquest, and probably a post-mortem, too.'

'You don't seem surprised,' said the doctor, looking up at him narrowly from under his rumpled grey eye-brows.

'No. I thought myself that it was all wrong. He wasn't ill. I've never known him really ill, nothing but seasonal colds, and flu, and things like that. I didn't see how he could possibly just stop living, like this. Can you tell what he really did die of?'

'It will take a post-mortem to say for certain; but yes, I can make a pretty close estimate. He died of a good large dose of one of the barbiturates, luminal or something like it. He's been dead several hours.'

They stood looking at each other for a moment in an exchange of thoughts which needed no words. Then Bill said: 'He had his coffee last night, as usual. I don't think he sat up late, I don't think he was working. But he drank his coffee. The tray's in the next room now, it hasn't been touched. That was right, wasn't it?' And after a momentary struggle with the wave of panic that rose in him like a high tide, he asked almost brusquely: 'I don't know the proper drill – who sends for the police, you or me?'

Estelle and Gerard were in the hall together when Bill came downstairs at the doctor's heels. They were silent, and they were not looking at each other. Gerard stood near the window, staring out into the garden; Estelle was in a chair by the hearth, with the morning paper spread open in her hands, but the intense nature of her stillness and concentration did not suggest that she was reading it.

'I'm sorry!' said Bill rather wearily, 'I'm afraid you've been shockingly neglected, I do apologise. But something pretty shattering has happened. I don't know if my aunt has told you already – Uncle Philip died suddenly in the night.'

It sounded curiously stilted to him, and completely unreal. Every time he said it or thought it, it hit him hard under the heart again, and made him gasp. It didn't seem to him that he could ever get used to it.

The paper crumpled sharply between Estelle's hands. Her eyes looked over it with a scared, wild gleam of violet light, animal in their alarm and defensive ferocity. But when the paper sank slowly into her lap her face was revealed in marble stillness, even her breath held for a moment. 'Dead?' she said in a whisper, not doubting, only, as it seemed, trying to grasp it, and her eyes flew to her husband. 'But how?' But it was clear that she was not putting the question to Bill, and he made no attempt to answer it.

Gerard, turning so that the light was behind him and his face obscured, stared with dropped jaw and almost incredulous frown and, having grasped the certainty of Bill's verdict, made appropriate noises of distress and dismay.

'How terrible! What a dreadful thing to happen, and what a shock for you! I can't tell you how sorry Estelle and I are to hear such sad news. If there's anything we can do to be of help – anything at all – please do count on us. Mrs Greville – she'll be arriving by train – could I—?'

'Rachel Pharamond is meeting her,' said Bill. 'Thanks, all the same! Will you excuse me for a moment? I have to telephone the police.'

He didn't know why he dropped the brutal fact in their laps like that, nor why he recoiled with so much distaste from Gerard Renaud's sympathy. Perhaps it had already become clear to his subconscious mind that someone in this household had poisoned Philip, and instinctively he was selecting for distrust the stranger simply because to look with doubt upon Mary, or the servants, was altogether too fantastic, as well as quite unbearable. He saw Gerard's heavy jaw sag still further in amazement and consternation, or a good imitation of both. But what did that mean? No one in this house could afford to be anything but amazed and concerned from now on. He went to telephone, leaving Dr Benson to meet the inevitable outcry.

'The police? But I don't understand! How can the police possibly come into the matter? You have examined Mr Greville, I take it, Doctor – a most tragic death, and a terrible shock for his wife, but is there really any ground for supposing it to be anything but natural?'

Estelle sat mute, her hands gripping the arms of her chair, her eyes flashing with desperate shrewdness from one face to the other, like an animal making a lightning estimate of the possible bolt-holes out of a dangerous situation. Grief, if she had for one instant had grief in her eyes, was already gone; among so many nearer preoccupations there was no longer any room for it. She could think as quickly as Gerard, and see as far.

'Gerard, I feel that perhaps we could at least relieve Mrs Greville of the burden of having guests at a time like this. She'll have more than enough trouble to face, without that. And I'm sure she'd much rather have just her own family about her. If we're not needed, we could drive back to town today, instead of on Tuesday. It might be the best way of helping.'

'I'm afraid,' said the doctor dryly, 'that it may be necessary for you to stay. It will be for the police to say if you can leave, and when.'

'The police?' Gerard moistened his grey lips, and his

eyes flickered for an instant to his wife's face, and were met by a look of wild, distrustful intelligence. 'But surely they can't suppose that my wife and I know anything about Mr Greville's death? The most casual of visits – a mere accident that we're here at all—'

'If Mr Greville's death is not the result of natural causes,' said the doctor patiently, 'and I can tell you here and now that that's extremely unlikely, then there are just three possibilities: accident, suicide and murder. Nothing about him ever suggested to me that suicide would be within his scope; to have an accident with – what I take to be the agency of his death – he would have to be in possession of it, and in the legitimate habit of taking it, which emphatically he was not. I'm his doctor, I know the full tale of the drugs I've ever prescribed for him, and they're precious few in any case, and this one isn't among them. And that makes the third possibility loom a little larger than is quite comfortable, Mr Renaud. The police have their job to do. They'll tell you when you can leave here – but I don't think it will be today.'

Gerard did not pursue the suggestion of leaving; he was perfectly aware that anxiety and indignation were to be dissembled at all costs. Instead, he asked at once: 'But what is it you think he's taken? What drug?'

'One of the barbiturates, probably luminal. Something I'm convinced he never took in his life before. I doubt if there's even any in the house.'

'Yes,' said Mary's quiet voice from the doorway, 'there is.'

She had come in unnoticed from the kitchen, and stood just within the room. She had been crying, and it

had done her good; her face was wretched but calm, with
the determined, competent, roused calm of someone
who has emerged successfully from an intense crisis. 'I
had luminal tablets once,' she said to the doctor, 'on a
prescription from your locum, when you were away in
hospital yourself – do you remember? It must be nearly
three years ago now. He gave me a bottle of fifty – I dare
say he was over-enthusiastic, he was that kind of young
man. I don't think more than a dozen or fifteen were
ever taken, but I can't try to guess how many there
ought to be in the bottle. It's so long since I even looked
at it.'

'And where is this bottle now?' asked Dr Benson.

'Gerard and I could hardly know anything about it,
could we?' Estelle put in rapidly. 'Only someone who
lived in the house could possibly know you had any such
tablets.'

The fight was on already, the fight to step back out of
the spotlight and leave someone else blinded in its glare.
Estelle would have no mercy and no scruples. Was she
more afraid than other people, or only quicker in realisation of danger? Bill, coming back from telephoning,
heard the note of resolute self-interest in her voice, and
wondered bitterly if he was soon going to be elbowing his
way past her towards the escape doors.

'They're in the bathroom cabinet,' said Mary, 'and
available to anyone who happened to look in there for a
styptic pencil or the iodine. There's no secret about
them, and they've never been under lock and key because
we've taken it for granted that everyone in the house was
an adult, and responsible. I dare say they ought to have
been locked up, but they never were.'

'Would you mind,' asked the doctor, 'if I took charge of them?'

'I should be very glad if you would. If, of course, they're still there.'

They were still there. Within two minutes the doctor came downstairs again, carrying the little bottle carefully in a folded handkerchief. It was that handkerchief, more than any other detail, that underlined the real state of the case. Bill stood staring at it, and his mind was recapitulating feverishly some broken echoes from Thursday evening, and fitting them together into the framework of this tragedy. '—it would mean getting hold of something lethal by strictly private means – but it needn't be something that left no trace, the traces would only end in mid air. Then all you would have to do would be to keep your nerve—'

'Look at it, Mary.' The doctor held out the little phial on the palm of his hand, still shielded by the handkerchief. 'Does it seem to you less full than it ought to be?'

'I don't know. I can't possibly say. Once the cotton-wool's out of the neck, you know, the bottle's already nearly half empty. At this half-way stage, ten tablets, more than ten, could be taken out, and still leave it looking much the same. I told you, I don't know how many there ought to be, and it would be wrong to start guessing.'

'These are two-grain tablets,' said the doctor musingly. 'Ten of them could—' He broke off, and wrapped the little bottle carefully in the handkerchief.

But there won't be finger-prints, thought Bill, in response to the doctor's unspoken suggestion. That's of the essence. Whoever took Philip's tip and killed him had the whole idea fresh in his mind, detective-story fashion, straight from the horse's mouth. He wouldn't forget about finger-prints; he had an expert tutor.

And I was there, too, he thought, remembering things he would have preferred to forget. I spent the last few days quarrelling with him, all the household knows it, the rector knows it, the doctor knows it. I wanted him to release my money, and he wouldn't, and everybody will think: 'It suits Bill much better to have Helen stepping into his trustee's shoes, he can get what he wants out of Helen.' Once I even said something absurd, in a temper, after he'd been making fun of me. 'Over my dead body!' he said, and I said— A wave of burning heat swept through him as he remembered what he had replied, like a spiteful child screaming: 'I hate you! I'll kill you!' when all it means is: 'I can't get my own way with you!' He didn't know whether he felt more frightened or ashamed, but the dull, miserable ache that filled his mind and heart did not seem to go with the fright part of his reactions.

The hum of the car turning in from the road, and the crunch of wheels on gravel, made them all spring round to look through the french windows, long before the car had time to make the circle of the house and enter their view.

'That will be the police,' said the doctor, almost with eagerness. For things mechanical the doctor had no ear at all; for the note of this engine was immediately recognisable to Bill as that of the rector's Ford.

'It's not the police,' he said, 'there hasn't been time. It's Helen!'

He plunged across the room impetuously, before any

175

of them could forestall him and make a hash of the unbearable business, which God knew was dreadful enough already. He sprang through the open french windows and down the steps into the garden, and ran to meet Helen as she stepped out of the car.

She was intensely pale, and yet he had never noticed her brightness so clearly. It was as if she were lit from within, incandescent with her ecstasy of anxiety and foreboding. Her eyes, beneath the lucid forehead, were wide in wonder and dread, and already seemed to be staring at tragedy, but with a superhuman tranquillity. She said: 'Bill!' on an almost inaudible breath, and extended her gloved hands to him in appeal, and he flew to take them, to put an end to that hopelessly pathetic gesture of theirs in mid air. He drew her by them closely, warmly against him, and shut his arms tightly round her, and held her like that all the time he was speaking to her, his cheek against her hair. She had left her foolish little white hat, and her handbag and scarf, in the car. Rachel, quietly gathering them up after her, watched the meeting with interest, and found it enlightening, as well as moving.

Poor Bill, she thought, I wonder if that's why he's been so mad to get away, miles away, a continent away. If it is, he hasn't an inkling of it himself, he thinks he feels towards her as a good son ought to feel – but it looks as if some bit of him, deep inside, has been uneasy for a long time, years maybe, feeling that there was something wrong in quality, something excessive, about his feelings towards his uncle's wife. And Philip's death hardly resolves that, does it? Poor Bill! She was proud of her detachment, but it did not prevent her from feeling a certain unpleasantly perceptible pain which did not, on the whole, appear to be entirely on Bill's behalf. No wonder he'd never paid any attention to girls of his own age, no wonder he couldn't even see them, with that blinding light in between.

'Darling,' said Bill, quite softly and slowly, putting into his voice all the molten affection that filled his heart to bursting, 'something terrible has happened while you've been away, and you must be very brave, and remember that we all adore you, and rely on you, and would do anything, anything in the world, to help you, or keep you from unhappiness. Please forgive me if I was wrong, I couldn't bear you to hear it from anyone but me, or anywhere but here, at home, where at least there'll be privacy for you, and little things left to comfort you. Darling – it's Philip. He – Helen, he—' He faltered, seeing her face sharpen into a crystal clarity and awareness, and her eyes fix suddenly on the open windows where the others had appeared one by one, all but the one for whom she looked.

'Philip!' she said, in a still, thoughtful tone, to herself rather than to him. 'I don't see him – he isn't here.' She drew herself erect in the boy's arms, and stared into his face; and in acknowledgement of his pain she even smiled a little. 'My dear, don't distress yourself so! If you can say it, I can hear it. Tell me – I shan't make it worse for you. Philip is—'

'He's dead,' said Bill very gently. 'We found him dead in bed this morning. When he didn't come down to breakfast we were worried, Mary and I, and she went to wake him, and he was dead. Dr Benson's here now. After he'd seen him he waited, because there's something more, you see, Helen, something wrong about the death. We think he'd taken some tablets that killed him in his sleep.' He almost wished to keep back the last blows, but while she stood so straight and composed in his arms, and watched him with that pale and resolute face, he could not affront her by hiding anything. 'We've had to call in the police. The doctor can't give a certificate. There'll have to be an inquest, to find out the real cause of Philip's death. Darling, you are not to think at all about that – we will take care of everything. Don't let any of the complications weigh on your mind, or make the thing ugly for you. Where you and Philip are concerned there's nothing ugly at all – it's just simply that you've lost him. He loved you as long as he lived, and he didn't even know he was leaving you, so for him there wasn't any ugliness or regret at all. And that's what matters.'

Where had he found this unaccustomed eloquence? Nothing but love could have made him so fluent. Even at a moment like this Helen was able to find something amusing, as well as infinitely touching, in the measure by which Bill had excelled himself, for she was smiling through unshed tears as she reached up and kissed his cheek.

'My dear, my dear!' was all she said for a moment; and then, drawing herself a little away from his supporting arms, which at once released her: 'I'll go to him. Don't worry about me, Bill – I shall be all right.' Her voice was remote but firm, it came clearly from steady lips. When she walked towards the french windows she looked neither to right nor left, and nobody ventured to intrude upon her loneliness, even with sympathy. Bill followed her at a respectful distance across the hall and up the staircase, and waited humbly outside Philip's door, in case she should need him.

Helen closed the door, and was alone with her husband.

Bill sat on the stairs and waited for what seemed a very long time, watching but not seeing the constrained movements, hearing but not comprehending the nervous and rare utterances, of the others down below. Rachel had come in, and was talking in low tones to Mary, there beside the window. In her short red duffle coat and slim grey skirt, with her dark fringe ruffled, she looked like an athletic schoolgirl, until you remarked the power and profundity of the face. Bill had never really looked at it before, but now it was perhaps the only thing he could see clearly in all the great room below, the only thing that had an authenticity of its own even at this extreme crisis, when all his senses were concentrated on that closed door which separated him from Helen in her grief. He didn't blame her for shutting him out with the rest; his distress was all for her, not for himself.

At the first touch of her hand at the door he was on his feet, ready to stay or go, to embrace and hold her or draw back and let her alone, just as she should wish. She came out of the room with a slow, composed step, closing the door behind her. Her face was in shadow, he saw only the immense luminous blueness of her eyes shining in the dimness, and then the softer glimmer of her pale face. She was perfectly calm. No, this was something quite different in quality, more than serenity; she was exalted. She looked at him with that glittering stillness, and said in a quiet, direct and level voice:

179

'A police car has just turned in at the gates, with two officers in it. You had better go down, Bill, and let them in.'

The police were in almost constant possession of Philip's study for three days. They interviewed, and questioned, and took finger-prints, and went over the events of Good Friday again and again with every member of the household; but they did not extract from anyone the gist of the conversation which had taken place on Thursday evening. Philip himself had given them all the most explicit instructions on how to deal with this situation. 'All you have to do is keep your nerve, admit nothing, know nothing, do nothing. The traces will end in mid air, among half a dozen people who shared the same opportunity.' Did the police even discover any of the possible motives that were thick in the air of the house? Bill had only realised them himself, had only grown sensitive to their implications, after the event, when he saw Gerard and Estelle staring at each other with bleak and ferocious hatred through their masks of solidarity and affection, as they stood together shoulder to shoulder against the world. Not out of love, that was certain! Out of self-interest. I will swear black white for you, because it is the only way I can hope to induce you to swear black white for me. I will know nothing, absolutely nothing, of any compromising relationship you may have had with Philip Greville, on the strict though unspoken understanding that you will suppress what you know about me. Nothing was ever said, no such bargains ever made in words; that was not necessary. These two understood each other as completely as they hated each other.

'We sat here for perhaps ten minutes after Miss Greville had said good night,' Gerard had said at his first interview, 'and then we went up to bed.'

'Together?'

'Of course, together.'

There had been no need for any prior agreement between them on this point. They had drawn together instinctively in the impregnable lie. No one had heard them quarrel, no one had seen them part. No one could prove they were lying, even if Bill, grown abnormally sensitive now to the stresses round him, vibrated in protest like a lie-detector when they made their flat statements.

And that left him, last to go up to bed that night, with no one to lie for him, or at least only by suppression. He had gone up the stairs alone, after the house was quiet; he had even hesitated for a long minute outside Philip's door, he had – oh, God, he'd touched the coffee-pot, he might have left distinguishable prints on it! He could have dropped luminal tablets into it easily enough; he could have taken them from the bathroom at any time that day or days beforehand, they were always available to him. So much for an opportunity. What about motive? The Renauds would know nothing, though they could not choose but know how the whole house had been uneasy with his fretting after escape, and how Philip had said flatly, in front of them all, that he would not, in any circumstances, let him have the means to go off to Canada with Lawson. Mary and Helen would not lie, perhaps, but they wouldn't volunteer any information on that subject unless they were asked, and if no one prompted the police in the first place they probably never would be asked. The household, with all its diverse personalities, was being forced into a solidarity of silence against the common enemy. Most people talk too much when the police are around, out of sheer nervousness; but these people had been tutored by Philip, and were schooled in the virtues of ignorance and silence.

And the servants were not resident in the house, to know all too well the affairs of uncle and nephew. They came in daily from the village, and went home in the afternoon. So only Bill himself could supply the police with the facts about his motive, short of some unforeseen disaster. He was going to have some strenuous lying to do, at least by implication.

When it came to the point, however, he did not actually have to lie about his relations with Philip; and that in itself was a revelation.

'You were on good terms with your uncle, Mr Grant?'

He had said: 'Yes,' even before he had time to consider, so natural and true did the affirmative seem. He spoke with a sudden half-smile of remembrance for Philip's many-sided personality, which had rendered life with him long ago so unpredictable, so stimulating, so much fun. 'We fell out sometimes,' he said, still remembering, and still smiling. 'I was fond of my own way, and he was an artist, and volatile, and the mixture was often explosive. The fireworks we generated were very handsome, but they never did any great harm.'

After that he had found himself sweating in the expectation that the next question would be: 'Was there anything in dispute between you recently?' And then he would have lied, because he was scared, because when it came to the point he simply didn't trust the law as completely as all that, because he didn't believe that innocent people are never convicted. But the next question was: 'Had your uncle any enemies, to your knowledge?' And he had said ruefully: 'He must have had one. But I don't know who that could be. I should have said he hadn't a real enemy in the world. There were lots of people he couldn't get on with, lots of people he quarrelled with, all the humbugs and the climbers and the sycophants and the poseurs – he couldn't bear them and they couldn't bear him. But they just kept out of his way. You don't kill people because you're incompatible with them, not unless you're forced to live with them – you just sheer off.'

The inspector had looked at him thoughtfully, and said at length: 'You're taking it for granted someone killed him? I don't recollect committing myself to any such opinion. We haven't got the inquest over yet, you know.'

'No, I know. But you did say that it's already established he died of luminal poisoning, and I don't quite see how that could have happened by accident.'

'You wouldn't, I take it, consider suicide as a possibility?'

Bill had shouted: '*No!*' to this, so scornfully that there was hardly any need to elaborate his rejection of the theory. But he did add, a shade startled by his own vehemence: 'He was a hundred per cent happy – well, say ninety, maybe no one ever does better than that – and two hundred per cent alive. But even if he'd been old, and decrepit, and ill, and lonely, he'd never have killed himself – not in any circumstances. It was just the flat opposite of everything in him.'

And then he had felt better, because it was true, and in some obscure way it was an obituary of Philip, and one he was glad to have uttered.

The inspector said resignedly to his sergeant, on the eve of the inquest: 'Every person in the house may have had a strong motive for wanting Greville out of the way, but we shall never know any of them, unless a miracle happens.' He had been reviewing the relationships involved in the case, and they were all apparently blameless. Greville, his wife, his sister and his nephew had lived amicably together for fifteen years, and there was no visible reason why they should change now. The other two were strangers, an old acquaintance – perhaps more? – of Greville's, and her husband, chance-met a few weeks ago, and invited for Easter. There was no one here, outside Hugonin's Mill, who knew anything at all about them; and no one in the other part of their life, it seemed, who knew anything about the Grevilles. The woman was interesting, very interesting, but the connection, as it stood, extremely tenuous.

'Opportunity,' said the sergeant, 'they all had – barring Mrs Greville, of course, she was a hundred miles away all that day. Miss Greville made the coffee, she was alone in the kitchen, she took the tray up herself. She's the one who had the tablets – I know they were where anyone could get at them, but she's the one most likely to think of them, because they were prescribed for her. But why in the world should she want to kill her brother? There's the boy Grant, he came back after seeing Miss Pharamond home, and found everybody else had already gone up to bed. He says himself the tray was still there. Naturally he says he didn't touch it, but he easily could have done, there was nobody else about by that time. But again, we don't know of any reason he had for wanting his uncle out of the way. Then the Renaud couple – they're out of it according to their evidence, they went up to bed together. Well, they're husband and wife, maybe you could say it's only natural they should give each other an alibi. Only in this case I can't say I get the impression of a devoted couple, exactly. In any case, we haven't a scrap of evidence that either of them had a motive for killing Greville. There *could* have been all sorts of grudges among them, but there's no sign of any.'

'The coffee in the pot was stiff with luminal,' said the inspector, 'as well as the dregs in the cup. Evidently the stuff was dropped into the pot – which is just about the most unlikely way in the world of committing suicide. The only prints on the pot are Greville's own, and those of Mrs Greville, who put the tray ready in the morning, and Miss Greville, who made the coffee at night. There's some trace of a hand-print round the belly of the pot, but nothing identifiable. The knob on the lid has no prints except Greville's and Miss Greville's, which is as it should be. Everything, in fact, is as it should be, except that a man's dead who ought to be alive. We don't even know for certain that the luminal that killed him came from that bottle, though it's a reasonable assumption, especially as the bottle is a dead blank where prints are concerned, which in normal circumstances it certainly wouldn't be. We don't, in fact, know anything for certain – except, as I said, that the poor devil's dead.'

'And none of the people involved knows anything for certain either,' said the sergeant sceptically.

'That could be genuine in all cases but one, of course.

Or it could be pure fright. Or it could be a case of every-body having *something* to hide. We'll stay close, and keep pegging away. Sooner or later somebody's nerve is going to give way.'

But nobody's nerve gave way. They were already fore-warned and forearmed against any such eventuality. Philip had had apt pupils.

Nothing new emerged at the inquest; nothing new was allowed to emerge. Only the awkward fact that the luminal had undoubtedly been administered in the coffee, in a manner very unlikely in a suicide and almost impos-sible to consider as an accident, prevented the jury from bringing in an open verdict. As it was, they were compel-led at last to agree on a verdict of murder against a person unknown. If Thursday's conversation on the subject of murder had been brought to their notice they might have reached the same conclusion in considerably less time and with fewer misgivings; but somehow that little discursion had fallen clean out of the memory of every person who had been present to hear it. Even the rector had seen fit to put it out of his mind, perhaps because it made contacts with the household at Hugonin's Mill too embarrassing, and he had come to rely on them too much to want to sever them now.

'A perfectly sound verdict,' said the inspector bitterly, 'and only four people to pick from, barring the extremely remote chance of some unknown intruder. And we're about as likely to be able to pick out the right one and bring it home to him – or her! – as we are to pan gold out of the mill-stream down there. If only they'd be a shade more talkative, at least one of them might say the wrong thing.'

But they preserved still their impenetrable reserve. After the brief, unelaborated answers he let the silences grow long and oppressive, but no one was shaken into rushing in to fill the gaps with indiscreet sound. Only Helen, immured from all other anxieties in her solitary and unobtrusive grief, talked, as he felt, naturally; but why should Helen, in any case, labour to contain what she knew, when she knew no more than he did? She alone stood clear of all the events of that Good Friday, with some millions of witnesses to testify to her whereabouts and her actions at the close of the evening, at least a hundred miles from the scene of the crime.

Permission had been given for Philip's funeral to take place, and two days after the inquest they buried him. Helen in her deep black stood by the graveside, in the heavy, reddish clay, and watched what was mortal of Philip lowered into the pit. Her face was veiled, but it would seem by the stillness of her hands, which were gripped together before her, and the composure of her slight body, that she did not weep. Bill stood beside her, his arm through hers. He was extremely pale, and looked tired and haggard, and more than his age, and his eyes followed the descent of the coffin with fascination and horror; but his composure matched Helen's. When they turned away from the grave Helen's enormous wreath of daffodils and tulips, all white and gold, was left shining radiantly in the mist and gloom of a dull day. Rachel watched them get into the car, just as the thin, cold rain of spring began to fall. She wondered if Helen had noticed how abruptly, during the past few days, Bill had completed his growing up.

*　　*　　*

The inspector came to see Helen the next day. He found her in Philip's study, assembling the mass of her husband's works, and collecting together all the letters and documents he had accumulated in the years of his celebrity. Bill, who had been helping her to sort out this material, took himself off as soon as the inspector arrived, and went down into the garden, leaving them to talk in privacy.

He didn't know what was the matter with him. He wished he could feel happier about the work in hand, as Helen, he was sure, took comfort in it. There ought to be a life of Philip Greville, by all means, he ought to be remembered; more than that, his memory ought to be celebrated with ardour; only somehow, when he saw that row of rather precious novels assembled, and the small honours put together, the little prizes which so delighted Helen's heart, the sum of it seemed so ludicrously and meanly inadequate to be Philip's memorial. And he thought, if I were writing a book about him, I don't think I should find it necessary to do more than mention those things; they hardly seem important enough even to go in at all. Philip was something quite different, something infinitely bigger. All the same, he was glad to see Helen occupied upon a darling project of her own, something that would keep Philip ever-present with her while she worked at it. She had grown more remote, more abstracted, more radiant and silent and still, since Philip was gone, as though she had her plans already made to go after him. Philip would have been vehement in disapproval. To him, life was for living.

Down by the pack-bridge the wet green trees leaned over angry brown water, swollen after the heavy rain. On the banks stood the Renauds, very close together, turned a little away from each other, as he had seen them constantly since Philip's death. They looked exactly like two swordsmen, not naturally allies but drawn together for mutual protection in a world of enemies, guarding each other's backs from treacherous assault. But when they exchanged glances he had seen their faces stiff with concealment, and their eyes looking out as through windows in a wall, anguished with mutual hate. They had been waiting for days now to get away, only to get away, to be allowed to go where they need no longer stand together in this enforced alliance which scarified them both, where they could discard the niceties of self-preservation, and tear each other to pieces. And yet he was sure, as sure as he was of their state now, that they had come to Hugonin's Mill tolerant of each other, rather bored and mischievous on her part, rather possessive on his, nothing worse than that. What had happened between them? That it had involved Philip he was quite sure. That one of these two had been the instrument of Philip's death he felt in his heart. Only there was nothing to show which, and no means of proving it.

They saw him approaching, and turned to face him with expectancy, almost with eagerness. They were waiting all the time for the words that would release them, and he might easily be the messenger.

'That was the inspector again, wasn't it?' Gerard asked without finesse. 'What did he want this time?'

'He's still with Aunt Helen,' said Bill. 'I left them to it.'

'How much longer does he think he can keep us here? My business is suffering. There's surely no need for us to stay here now – if he wants us again he could very easily find us.'

'If he sees fit to take the restrictions off us,' said Bill, 'no doubt Helen will be glad to let you know as soon as possible.'

'It will certainly be a relief to her, too,' agreed Gerard, noting the hint of asperity in this rejoinder. 'I suppose you'll probably be off yourself,' he went on, watching the boy with wary curiosity. 'The money, I take it, won't be a problem now.'

'Does he really think *I* did it?' thought Bill. 'And for that reason? If he means that, then he can't have done it himself, can he? Or is it only that, precisely because he did it himself, he finds it expedient to drop these subtle indications that he believes it was my doing? And would he bother to put on a show of that kind for me, after the way we've all lied the last few days, either explicitly or implicitly?' He hesitated, wondering how to reply to the question in any case, whether it was honest or whether it wasn't. The project had dwindled so far into the back of his mind that he found it an effort to care now whether he went or stayed; the excision of Philip from his life dwarfed everything else.

However, he was absolved from having to make any answer. Estelle's attention had been diverted by a movement between the shrubberies, far away up the long green vista of lawns; and where she looked Gerard instantly looked, too.

'Ah, here's Mrs Greville now. He must have left already. Whatever he had to say, it hasn't taken him long to say it.'

Helen came over the wet grass, slender and frail in her

dress of unrelieved black, which rendered her gleaming fairness more ethereal than ever. If she had news, it did not show in her face, which was calm, serene and still. It seemed strange to Bill that she could be so unmoved by the stresses round her. She had not, it was true, the unworthy motives all the rest of the household had for wanting Philip's death to remain an unsolved mystery; but at least she ought to have cared, one way or the other, that so many creatures of her own kind should be living precariously from day to day in fear and pain. It wasn't like her not to care.

'You needn't have run away, Bill,' she said. 'The inspector stayed only a few minutes.' She looked into Gerard's face, and very faintly and coolly she smiled, aware of his agony of impatience. 'He apologised, Mr Renaud, for keeping you here so long. I'm sure you understand that he was only doing his duty. But now he says that we can all consider ourselves free to move again. You may leave Hugonin's Mill whenever you wish.'

They drew breath as one creature, relaxing for a moment even from mutual hate into the one blessed conviction that they had survived it, that it was over. They hardly waited to gloss over their agony of relief with civilities, but after the barest of renewed protestations and regrets and excuses flew to pack their belongings and prepare for departure. Helen watched them go with the palest and politest of smiles.

Chapter 3

'I suppose,' said Bill, drawing nearer to Helen's shoulder, 'that means, in effect, that the police have given up.' And suddenly the thought held no pleasure or relief for him, as he had expected, but was only a gross wrong committed against Philip. He was in an odd state, he felt it himself, still scared, still feverish to have the crisis past and be able to breathe again without constantly wondering if the history of his last quarrel with Philip would not somehow leak out, and yet even more preoccupied with unexpected regrets and remembrances in which he sometimes lost sight of his own danger. How many things there had been to like about Philip, and how terrible, how unjust it was that his death should be reduced simply to a source of danger to the survivors. He wanted to express his sense of guilt to somebody, he wanted a confessor for this uncontrollable late fondness that could distract him even from the motions of self-preservation.

'I don't think they ever give up,' said Helen. 'They know where to lay hands on us all, whenever they want us.'

'You know what I meant. They've given up expecting any success. I know they'll go on trying. Helen, it's only sometimes that I realise that somebody *killed* Philip – really killed him, put an end to him, all that life, and gaiety, and warmth he had. Do you know what's the most terrible thing about it? – that I've been so frightened about my own position that I could hardly see how terrible it was that Philip should be robbed like that. It makes me so ashamed! Whoever killed him ought to pay for it to the limit. It wasn't only a crime against him, it was a crime against the world! And yet all I've had room for in my mind was the worry of whether I should be suspected, whether somebody would tell that I'd fallen out badly with him over the money and was desperate for a way of getting my hands on it. Helen, it's all so wickedly wrong!'

'Bill, my dear!' Helen put a hand on his arm, and lifted her beautiful face, smiling at him with soft, superficial tenderness. 'There's nothing to worry about now. Of course you were afraid for yourself! Did you expect to be superhuman? Don't you think Philip would have understood? You'll be able to make a clean break now. If it's too late to go with your friend to Canada, there'll be some other opportunity. And the money will be at your disposal whenever you need it – you know I won't stand in your way.'

He was aware of an embarrassing check, as though he had opened the wrong door. Did Helen still see that as of the slightest importance? He could hardly remember now the feeling of urgency he supposed it must have had for him some days ago. But he could hardly blame Helen for not knowing that, could he? None the less he was aware of frustration, as though language had failed him and he could no longer communicate.

'It isn't that, I'm not worrying about that. I only wish we hadn't been at cross purposes about it, that's all it means now. But I keep thinking how wrong it is that Philip should be dead. He had years and years of life in him, he'd have lived to be a hundred – he couldn't have helped it, he was so in love with living. Someone just cut him off, like cutting grass, like swatting a fly! *Philip!* And all I could think about was that I might come under suspicion myself! And now there's no way of making up for it. He's dead. I can't go to him and say: "All right, you old devil, you were right and I was wrong, and I'm sorry." It's too late. He's gone.'

'I know how you feel, Bill,' she said gently. 'I understand very well. But death isn't such an infinite disaster. Nor life such a wonderful thing to lose.'

He saw with consternation, with a hideous constriction of the heart, that she didn't understand at all, that she was worlds away from knowing how he felt. 'It is! It is! If you despise life you despise everything – God most of all! Philip knew how to value it! Philip's values were all sound and true!' He didn't know how to express what he had in his heart, while she stood smiling at him so softly and distantly, her blue eyes large and kind and vague upon his distress. She wasn't really with him. Good God, she wasn't even listening, except with the smooth surface of her mind, on which his laboured phrases made hesitant, unexpressive ripples, and then left it still and calm. She was immured within her own world, looking out at him. He felt for a way in to her, but there was none; he had never been so alone in his life. She looked at him with affection, touched him briefly on the cheek with her small, delicate hand, stretched upward quickly, and kissed him. He felt cold, confused and miserable, but his tongue could not find any better words, and he was hopelessly silent.

'Darling, do you think there's anything you can tell me about Philip that I don't already know? He was my husband, and I loved him. Some other time we'll have a long talk about him – yes, Bill, I mean it, I need it too. But now I've got to go in – here's Dr Benson coming to see me. No, it's nothing out of the way, don't worry, only a routine examination.'

The doctor had left his car on the road and cut across the field to the pack-bridge, as he always did. He came across the treacherous, mossy stones at his usual brisk half-walk, half-trot, greeted Bill with a bright, shrewd glance, and swept Helen away with him through the garden and into the house.

Baulked of the humble, bewildered apology he had certainly been about to offer to Helen, for what precise fault he himself hardly knew, Bill sat kicking his heels on the arm of the stone seat by the river-bank and moodily watched them go. It shamed and frightened him that when Helen had stated her claim to know her husband through and through, he had suffered a sudden vision of a row of slim novels and three or four literary prizes arrayed on Philip's empty desk. What was the matter with him? If it was nothing but the hangover from personal grief and fear, he had better snap out of it at once. And it couldn't be anything more. He must be ill if he was beginning to think his sense of values more reliable than Helen's!

Rachel found him still sitting there when she crossed the field from the village and picked her way with long, sure strides over the uneven stones of the bridge. She had a shopping bag on her arm and the parish magazine in her hand; he couldn't help smiling at the sight of her, the girl herself seemed to have so little possible connection with her errands.

'I know!' said Rachel, by no means offended by the grin. 'I suppose I do look about the least probable deliverer of parish magazines you could imagine – but it gets me out of the house.' She halted by his stone bench, and looked down at him with a considering frown. 'I hear the Renauds are off.'

'The grapevine's still working well up to schedule, then. The inspector only left here about ten minutes ago. Yes, he says they can leave. They're busy throwing their things together now. They can't get away from us fast enough. I suppose the village doesn't claim to know which of us actually did it?'

'If they know, they haven't confided in me. Probably I'm held to be connected with the house, and therefore not on the delivery list for the more intimate rumours. I think it's regarded as unlikely that anybody'll ever be charged.'

Bill heard himself saying, to his own amazement: 'You didn't ever consider it as a possibility that *I'd* done it?' He hadn't meant to ask her anything of the sort, as far as he knew; and the tremor of anxiety beneath his carefully light tone deepened his astonishment. He covered his momentary consternation by moving up to make room for her beside him. 'Sorry, I'm an oaf! Do stay for a bit – I can't get anyone to listen to me seriously.'

With composure Rachel sat. 'Did you want me to take that question seriously? Then, no, I never entertained the idea that you could have done it.' She was entirely grave, her dark eyes met his squarely, and he was strangely comforted. He didn't know exactly why. It was perhaps that he felt something in her which had been in Philip too, and if she had fully and fairly understood that none of his rages against Philip had ever had in it anything secret, permanent or venomous, then probably Philip had always known as much and always been, in the obscure way which really mattered, profoundly at peace with him.

Almost fearfully, in case the answer should be disastrously wrong, he asked: 'Why did you feel so sure of that?'

'Because you and Philip loved each other very much,' said Rachel, 'and that's tough enough to stand all the pressures either of you could ever put on it.' She named love as directly and fearlessly as she had once named God, conceiving it as either adolescent or hypocritical to be embarrassed by the grandeur of either name. And the answer was not wrong; it was so beautifully, mercifully right that he felt all his tensions relax into trembling gratitude.

'Yes, I did love him! I hardly realised it myself, I'd never thought much about it until now – you don't think about these things. But I did! I hope he knew it.'

'He knew it,' said Rachel. 'What's come over you, to start digging over this particular ground? You haven't been suffering from a sense of estrangement, have you, just because you happened to be fighting a minor skirmish with him when he was killed? Accidental complications like that wouldn't upset Philip's judgement, you needn't worry.'

'It wasn't only that. It was that first, but not only that. It was the losing sight of him afterwards – being unable to feel anything except fright for myself, when I ought to have been feeling anger for him. It seemed to set him at such a distance from me—'

'It wouldn't,' said Rachel with conviction. 'He'd stick by you all the more if you were scared, and disgusted with yourself for being scared. It was heroes Philip was sceptical about.'

'You're sure,' said Bill, dazed by the fervour of his own relief, 'that you're not just trying to be nice to me?'

'I'm not thinking about you. I'm thinking about Philip. Even he had done a few things he wasn't proud of.' She gave him a quick, thoughtful look, and checked herself there. Very deliberately she said, watching him with sympathy at every word: 'Has it occurred to you, Bill, that there's only one person who seems to have no curiosity at all about the cause of Philip's death? This case is going to fade away gradually, as far as we can see, leaving a permanent shadow on everyone – except Helen. Isn't it odd that she, the only one patently innocent, the one most wronged, should show no preoccupation at all with the question of who killed her husband? Especially as he was her creation!'

Bill had lifted his head from his hands and was staring at her doubtfully, already disturbed by the seriousness of her tone, and remembering, only too evidently remembering, the reserve with which she had always contemplated Helen.

'What do you mean?' He was ready to spring into resentment at a word.

'Well, wasn't he? The Philip who operated here was a

Philip she'd made. It was she who shrank him to fit, down from the wild, lavish, generous creature he was, into her domesticated novelist, with his small accomplishments that he regretted and disliked so much. You heard what he said about his work, that night. Believe me, Philip wasn't joking – or if he was, it was a double-edged joke. Wouldn't you have thought Helen would have felt God's own indignation at seeing her creation cut off? Well, you've seen her! She doesn't even show any desire to know who killed him.'

Bill said, stiffening formidably: 'I don't know what you're getting at! I know you've never liked Helen. What's the matter, are you jealous of her, or something?'

Rachel gave him a long, considering and slightly belligerent stare of her dark eyes. 'In case it makes it easier for you, I don't mind admitting that I used to be. I was in love with Philip, terribly in love, when I was sixteen. He knew all about it – Philip always did. That's how we became such friends, once I'd got over not being able to be more. If you like to think I've still got it in for Helen because of that, of course you can. It remains true that she isn't at all preoccupied with the problem of who killed him. People act like that, Bill, only when they know already.'

Bill sprang up from the stone bench, trembling violently, and stood over her with a face convulsed with bewilderment and distress. 'What's wrong with you? Why do you always have to confuse everything? What makes it such fun for you to go round kicking over all the standards other people live by? Do you just *enjoy* overturning things?'

Rachel looked at him for once with a curiously vulnerable helplessness, and shook her head. It must have been an optical illusion that her lips quivered. 'No, I don't know that I enjoy it. But things may need overturning,' she said defiantly, 'if they've been standing on their heads from the beginning.'

Bill took her by the arm, and jerked her to her feet to face him. 'What did you mean, about Helen behaving as if she knows? I've got to know what you meant!'

'Exactly what I said, of course. What do you think I meant?' Rachel freed herself with a strong turn of her arm, but without any anger, and without drawing away from him. Looking over his shoulder she said, in a low voice: 'Look out, Helen's coming down the lawn with Dr Benson.'

He looked round quickly, half-suspecting a trick to deflect his anger, until he remembered that it was with Rachel he was dealing. Helen and the doctor were walking slowly, and deep in conversation, and not yet so near that they must have observed the two people beside the bridge. Bill found himself very reluctant to meet anyone just then, least of all Helen. He had to know what Rachel had on her mind, he had to get things clear in his own. What was the use of trying to pretend, even to himself, that Rachel was the sole author of this confusion which filled him?

'Don't go – you mustn't go yet, you've got to explain yourself. Here, come away from here!' He caught at her hand, in a gesture singularly different from that fierce grip on her arm a moment ago, and drew her back into the trees, the wet branches slithering past their shoulders. She could easily have pulled free from him, but this time she did not attempt it. They parted the bushes together until they were hidden from the path, and then stood still, looking back, for fear their rustling movements should betray their childish flight. The doctor would be leaving, as he had come, by this short cut over the bridge. A few minutes, and both he and Helen would be gone, and Bill and Rachel could resume their interrupted conflict. In the meantime they stood almost breast to breast, still hand in hand, looking at each other fiercely, and keeping an aching silence.

Helen and Dr Benson came down side by side, strolling without haste, to the river-bank. The doctor kicked a pebble from the path into the creaming brown flood, and said: 'One more rainstorm, and you'll have it out on the grass here. It looks as if I shall have to drive round to the front door next time I come.' And after a short pause he resumed, as though there had been no break in subject, and with the driest of voices: 'So to all intents and purposes it's all over.'

'It doesn't necessarily follow,' said Helen gently. 'But I really think it may be all over. I expect we shall still see the police from time to time, but I doubt if anything new will turn up now, and it's clear they don't think they have enough to justify a charge against anyone at the moment.'

'That doesn't trouble you?'

'Do you think it should?' she asked in the same tranquil tone.

'That depends entirely on your viewpoint, I suppose. Personally, perhaps from proximity, I feel rather strongly about poisons, and the people who use them, and I should be glad to see Philip's murderer brought to justice.'

The two in the bushes had not meant to listen; in the first

place they had merely been telling off the words they heard like beads, measuring out the time until the other two should depart and leave them free to emerge again. Only gradually did meaning enter into the exchanges. But now they were listening in a mutual guilt and shamelessness which drew them still closer together. They were taut, straining their ears; and his eyes were on the glimmer of Helen's fair hair and serene face as it appeared and disappeared between the stirring leaves, and Rachel's eyes were on him.

Helen was smiling; he could see the soft curve of her mouth and the silent dimpling of her cheek. She had halted by the bridge, the doctor close beside her; but in spite of the constant murmur of the water, the wind, blowing from the west, brought their voices clearly to the ears of the two who stood listening.

'Since it is all over,' said the doctor, 'may I ask you a peculiarly intimate question, Helen?'

'Of course?' she said, surprised

'How did you manage it?'

'I don't understand you,' said Helen, after a moment of blank silence. 'How did I manage what?'

'How did you kill Philip?'

If he had raised his voice, or in any way marked in his manner the extravagance of the thing he was suggesting, Bill would have cried out then and gone crashing through the bushes to confront him. But it was said so dryly and dully that for a moment he really did not understand, the sense of the words would not penetrate. Rachel saw the slow beginning of horror and indignation in his eyes, saw the hectic flush mount his face like a wave, and his lips open; and she put up her free hand and clamped it sharply over his mouth. It was not that she wanted to force him to hear further, it was rather that, whatever followed, he would not be able to bear the dubious memory of this challenge if he prevented Helen from answering now. It could not be left there, it had to be finished. She held him hard against her, and something in him acknowledged the force of her appeal and acceded to it. He was still, and when she took her hand away he did not cry out. The moment, in any case, the only possible moment for revealing themselves, was already lost.

Helen had not moved. She was no longer smiling, but her face retained its pale serenity. She stood looking at the doctor long and thoughtfully, and at length she said: 'I notice that you don't ask me why.'

'No need,' said the doctor, 'I know that already. I'm the only person who's in a position to know it. You killed him because you know, as I know, and as no one else knows, that your heart is in such a condition that you may drop dead at any moment, and can't in any case live long. You killed him because you couldn't bear to think of him living on after you, and enjoying life without you.'

And Helen smiled; radiantly, contemptuously, proudly, she smiled into the old man's face. The young man, rigid as an icicle between Rachel's hands, and almost as cold, stood with a motionless, shocked face staring between the branches. He already knew that the horrified, incredulous denial for which he had waited would never come; the moment for it was past. If it came now, who could believe in it?

'How little you know me!' said Helen. 'After all these years, how very little you know me! I killed him because without me he would have gone to pieces, and that was something I couldn't allow to happen. Do you think I've forgotten what he was in the old days, before I married him? Do you think *he* had forgotten? If he could have known how soon I was to leave him, he'd have begged me to save him from slipping back into that decline and fall. I spared him the pain of knowing, but I have saved him. I couldn't go away and leave my work unfinished.'

'What you mean,' said the doctor with a bitter, resigned smile, 'is that you couldn't go away and leave him free to live, and work, and love as he pleased. You couldn't trust him not to marry again, and it was inconceivable to you that another woman should ever take your place. It was Mrs Renaud, wasn't it, who made up your mind for you? And you needn't have worried, my dear Helen, you needn't have worried at all! Philip's conception of love was something quite different from yours, and far more tragic. I've known him a long time. There never would have been anyone but you for Philip again, living or dead. That was his tragedy. But he'd have lived without you, oh, yes, and enjoyed what was left, enjoyed it to the full – so perhaps, according to your lights, you were still justified.'

He had been all this while staring into the river; now he lifted his grizzled head and shrunken, disillusioned face, and looked at the fair beauty of Helen shimmering in the watery sun. 'Did you think that Philip shared your values, because he surrendered to them for your sake? Do you think he liked the kind of tribute you asked of him, because he brought it to you so faithfully? Do you know what he once said to me, Helen? He said: "I'm the only person in the world, except you, who's ever seen through Helen. And they say love is blind!" '

She was impervious. She smiled still, her pure pallor not even marred by the slightest flush. 'I don't believe you! I knew Philip through and through, it was I who taught him to realise the best that was in him. Without me he would have slipped back again into the waste from which I took him. I've done what I had to do! If it is a sin, I'll answer for it.'

'If what you have done is a sin,' said the doctor grimly, 'you'll have to answer for it. And by our more worldly standards that could mean standing trial for murder.'

'If you are threatening me,' said Helen with angelic calm and patience, 'may I remind you that you have no witness to what I have just said?'

'Don't be afraid, I am neither God nor the law. I'm willing to leave you to those two – if one of them lets you slip through its fingers, I don't think the other will. You're condemned to death, and Philip's dead, what more can we ask? In any case, for his sake, one couldn't touch you. One can only go on serving you dispassionately for the rest of your life, and feel – forgive me! – unspeakably relieved when you die. No, I'm not thinking of taking any action. I merely wondered how you did it, from a hundred miles away.'

In a matter-of-fact tone, without any embarrassment whatever, Helen told him. Her confidence was impermeable by shame or doubt; she needed nothing from him or anyone, she *knew* she was justified.

'It was all very simple, Philip had shown me what to do. I was the first to go up to bed that Thursday evening, if you remember. I went straight to the bathroom, and took a number of tablets from Mary's little bottle in the cabinet there. I don't know exactly how many, I didn't count them. Nobody had used them for a long time, I felt sure nobody would know how many there ought to be. I held the bottle with a face tissue, so as not to touch it with my fingers. Then I went to bed. I knew Philip intended to work late, so he wasn't likely to disturb me for some time. When I was sure everyone else was asleep, I went down the back stairs – it's one of the advantages of old houses like this, that they have back ways – and in the kitchen I melted a little gelatine, and crushed the tablets and mixed them into it, and dropped the white cream with a spoon on to the petals of the white flowers in the base of the black coffee-pot. The gelatine congealed very quickly on the cold porcelain, and the rims of the petals held it, and when it was set no one could have guessed there was anything different about the pot. But of course the hot coffee would melt it almost immediately. Then, when it was ready, I went back to bed. And in the morning I put Philip's tray ready for the evening myself. There was nothing odd about that – Mary was used to my wanting to do things for him myself. The only odd thing is that I felt it to be necessary. He always had the same pot. I could have left it to Mary, and everything would have happened in exactly the same way. But somehow I felt I couldn't leave anything to chance. And I went to London and gave my recital. That was my fare-well to him – everything I sang was chosen for him – but you wouldn't understand that. And he drank his coffee, and went to sleep with my image in his eyes and my voice in his ears, and died in his sleep, intact, at his peak, safe from ever slipping back again. I say I saved him. You say I murdered him.'

'What do you expect me to call it?' said the doctor.

'Euthanasia? What do you think Philip was, a sick domestic pet? – a Mongol child?'

'I loved him, and I intended to keep him from violation.'

Her voice was high and secure; she *knew* herself to be without reproach.

'I think,' said Dr Benson, setting foot slowly on the mossy stones of the bridge, 'that you had better begin to feel the same preoccupation with your own conscience that you've felt hitherto with Philip's – before it's too late.' And he turned his shoulder abruptly upon her, and crossed with sudden, hurrying steps into the field. Helen stood for a moment where he had left her, and then, with some impulse to justify herself further, after all, walked after him to the middle of the bridge. But there she gave up the idea of pursuit. Perhaps he did not matter enough to her, perhaps she restrained herself because even to assay self-justification was an admission that she had doubts of her own, and she was unwilling to concede that she entertained any. Whatever the reason, she checked herself with a little, resigned shrug, watching the small, elderly figure for a few minutes as he stumped up the slope of the wet meadow. Then she turned, and began to retrace her steps.

Bill was standing on the bank, the bushes quivering behind him, staring at her with a face quite expression-less with shock. He had plucked himself out of Rachel's restraining arm, moving with the frenzied calm of shock, and she had let him go, following at his shoulder with eyes wide and wary for the moment when the ice would break. He stood in the wet emerald grass, staring at Helen as though he had never seen her before. At the suddenness of the apparition she halted for a moment, for once at a disadvantage. Then her face quivered into lively tenderness and pity for him; she had not meant him to learn the truth in this way.

'Bill!' There was no need even to wonder how much he had overheard, it was all there in the first struggling agonies of the stunned eyes as he came back to life. 'I'm glad, Bill! I'm glad you know! I hadn't meant you to find out this way, but it's done, and I'm glad. I'm not afraid that *you'll* fail to understand!'

She had recovered herself, she was coming towards him, smiling gently, confidently at him, holding out her arms to him. She expected him to walk into that proffered embrace and allow himself to be calmed and comforted. That was how she had always lulled his mind to sleep, and it had never failed her yet.

'Don't touch me!' cried Bill hoarsely, throwing up his arm to strike her hands away. 'Don't come near me! You killed Philip! *You!*'

'Bill, darling! I know it's been a shock to you—' She waited, her hands still hovering, grieved but sure of her dominance.

'Keep off! Don't touch me! You're a devil! No, you can't be a devil, devils know what they are, and you don't even *know*! You think you're *good*! And, my God, you made us all think you good! What's the matter with us all? How do we come to have everything the wrong way up? When I think of the years I've adored you, and been dazzled by you, and taken you for a saint! *You!*' he shouted, trembling violently. 'You, with your cool, small, self-conscious, self-centred virtue— And Philip— You think you *redeemed Philip*! My God! He

209

was human, he had his faults, but they were all large, warm ones, like him, better than all your damned virtues. *He was* good! He was honest, and generous, and loyal, he made people feel brave and gay – he wasn't capable of meanness. And you thought you could improve on that! You still think it! I wish I could think you were mad, but you're not mad – you're only a monster of vanity!'

His voice failed him for a moment, and dimly through the thunder in his ears he heard her appalled and pitying whisper of: 'Bill, my poor darling!' She was incurably sick, nothing could penetrate her armour of complacency. He took a violent step towards her, wild with frustration.

'You think you've done something fine! You murdered Philip – murdered him twice over, once when you scaled him down to your measure, and once when you put him to sleep, like a decrepit tom-cat, rather than let him outlive you and grow again. You killed him devoutly, and you expect the heavens to open and drop a halo on you— If there was a grain of truth anywhere in you, you'd know that you're damned, damned, damned!'

Rachel stretched out a hand to take hold of him and drag him back, but after all she arrested the movement. She was standing face to face with a horrible warning against trying to shape or influence anyone. He was a man, he had a right to his own actions and reactions. Even when he lunged forward with a wild gesture towards the bridge, Rachel did not touch him.

Helen's smile, which had not lost its confidence even before his last outburst, wavered at last; her soft, coaxing advance hesitated, shuddered, and swerved uneasily aside. She was out of reach of every other emotion that might have shattered her calm, but it seemed she was not out of reach of fear. The smoothness and beauty of her face seemed to break suddenly into fragments, like smashed glass, in a disintegration which was unpleasant to see; and more terrible than the terror itself was the ludicrous disbelief, that this malleable child whom she had raised in her own image should be proof against her now. She had managed him so dexterously through so many crises which seemed to her more extreme than this. Yet she recognised in Bill's convulsed and outraged face the end of her dominion. The sweep of his long young arm wiping the air before his eyes clean of her, a symbolic gesture of repudiation, appeared to her as the threat of a blow. Her imagination, like her virtue and her values, was limited to material things.

She uttered a whimpering cry, almost voiceless, as though pure surprise had paralysed her vocal cords. Her hands went up to ward him off, thrusting at the air between them, though he had already halted, yards short of touching her. She made a lame, stumbling leap back from him, and her feet slithered in the wet moss at the edge of the bridge. She uttered a scream that echoed back from the curtain of trees and coursed along the swollen water. Bill gave a cry that echoed hers, and sprang forward to try and catch her as she fell, but her silken sleeve ran through his fingers like rain. Then she was in the river, and for a moment swept under by the strong current below the bridge. She came up as an inert drift of black dress and fair, floating hair, rolling and turning in the eddies, her white hands limp as leaves. There was no movement in her now that was her own; the mill-stream animated her, and that was all.

Bill had leaped over the rim after her almost before she vanished from sight. The stream was hardly deep enough for swimming at any time but the spring spate, and even now its appearance of ferocity was something of an illusion. But he had hard work to keep his feet against the drag and impetus of the water, and even when he had drawn the drifting body into the shelter of his own he had much ado to control its dead weight. The small, fair face, blue and still in unconsciousness on his arm, moved him again with treacherous memories of beauty, the wet gold hair plastered against his sleeve clung like the recollections of the past. Irresistible fondness tore at his heart again. You cannot be sick with love for someone for fifteen years and be cured in a moment, even by methods as drastic as the knife; even amputations ache afterwards.

He gathered her into his arms, and brought her laboriously to the bank, and Rachel was there ankle-deep in the froth and rubbish of high-water to help him lift her up the slope of grass. He tugged off his wet jacket and rolled it up as a pillow for the streaming head.

'Helen!' He shook her, chafed her cheeks and her hands, took her by the chin and turned her face to one side, so that the water could run out of her lips. She did not stir.

Dr Benson, coming down the field and over the bridge at a headlong run, saw the sliding green marks in the moss, and grasped the reason for the scream which had dragged him back from his car. The two young people were kneeling over Helen on the grass, the boy working hard at artificial respiration. The doctor reflected sardonically that the exercise might at least do Bill good, in his present sodden condition, and forbore from remarking at once that it was almost certainly useless to Helen. They looked up at him with wild relief, since he was the one person who already knew so much that he could be allowed to hear everything.

Rachel scrambled aside to make room for him. Bill surrendered his patient to the accomplished old hands, and put back the streaming hair from his forehead. 'She isn't breathing – it doesn't seem to have any effect.'

The doctor turned Helen's limp body over, drew down her arms, opened one eyelid with a finger-tip.

'She can't have drowned,' said Rachel, 'there wasn't time. She wasn't in the water more than a minute or two, Bill went in after her like a flash.'

'No, she didn't drown. It was a foregone conclusion her heart wouldn't stand up to a shock like that. Fright, the fall, and the cold plunge killed her. Exactly how did it happen?'

It was Rachel who told him, in the fewest possible words. 'We were in the bushes when you came down with her, and we heard everything. We didn't hide for that purpose, it just happened like that. When you'd gone, we came out. She tried to carry it off, but this time it didn't work. When Bill made a move towards her – but he was nowhere near her, really – she jumped backward, and slipped there on the edge, and fell in. I think she thought he was going to hit her.'

'Maybe I was,' said Bill, staring at the translucent blue face motionless in the grass, 'I don't know!' He began to shiver with reaction and cold, and clenched his teeth to stop them from chattering. She was still beautiful. Reduced to a helpless thing under the doctor's probing hands, tumbled about in the soiled brown water and the wet and trodden grass, she was still beautiful. He could almost understand how she had been able to blind him for so long, and others with him. 'And I can't even remember her singing!' he burst out, shutting his eyes against the vision of that face uplifted in ecstatic and agonised song in the television screen, making a ceremony of self-worship, with music by Bach, out of the mean and treacherous murder of her husband. 'She's even spoiled that! She's spoiled everything!' A sense of horror filled him, because he found himself suddenly so near to her attitude, so perilously near to her crime. He was afraid he had been in her enervating shadow too long, and would never be free of her. 'I killed her!' he said, quaking with the cold of his sodden clothes in the chilly spring air. His teeth began to chatter uncontrollably. 'It was my fault! I killed her!'

Rachel put a hand on his shoulder with surprising strength and considerable exasperation, and shook him so roughly that he almost lost his balance, and was moved to spring indignantly to his feet to face her. 'Don't be a fool,' she said roundly. 'You never touched her, and you never would have touched her. If you don't know it, I do. For God's sake don't *you* start deluding yourself, leave that to the Helens! It wasn't from you she was trying to get away, it was from the mirror you held up to her, and the face she saw was her own, and none of your making. Don't start hiding behind a guilt you haven't a shadow of a right to.'

The momentary flash of reminiscent, angry dislike

died out of his eyes as he looked at her. She, at least, was real, at times irritatingly so, but always reassuringly. Something like the gleam of a harassed but genuine smile visited his face for a moment, and the first flush of natural colour returned to his smudged cheeks. He looked down again at the doctor, and asked quietly: 'What have we got to do about it? Must we tell the police? I suppose we must.'

'My dear boy, that's a matter of simple justice to yourself and Mary, as well as the Renauds. Yes, the police will have to know. It needn't worry you, the case will never come into court now. There may not even have to be an inquest, if they're satisfied with your statements and mine, and I see no reason why they shouldn't be. The cause of death won't be in dispute. No, they'll probably be content to make it known that the Greville case is closed to their satisfaction. A wasteful business,' he said with bitterness, clambering slowly to his feet, 'but an economical ending. No sensations, no loose ends, no immunity.'

He looked round at them suddenly, and frowned at Bill's dripping condition as though he saw it for the first time. 'Are you out of your wits, boy? Get inside and get those wet clothes off at once, unless you want pneumonia. Go on, go and ring up the police – tell them I'm waiting here until they come.'

Startled into obedience by the brusqueness of his tone, they turned at once, and set off up the slippery lawns at a rapid walk; and, as they went, by mutual consent they broke into a run. It began merely as a means of reaching the house the sooner, but in a few seconds it had become the running of children let out of school, of creatures newly relieved of a burden and intoxicated by their own lightness; and just as they reached the crest of the rise Bill, finding himself outrunning the girl, checked for a moment to stretch out a hand to her, and she caught at it, and they matched their speeds and went with linked hands out of sight.

The doctor watched them go, and the sight seemed to him infinitely reassuring. When he looked down again at the body of Helen it seemed already to have dwindled and grown more insubstantial.

'Well, you were always apt,' he said to her, wryly smiling. 'You know, don't you, what the village will say, since they won't have the details at their disposal – for I'll be very surprised, Helen, if the police feel it necessary to go to the bother of holding an inquest, just to prove that you fell into an icy-cold stream and not unnaturally died of myocardial failure. Your timing was always excellent. Here it is, the day after the funeral, and the widow in her deep mourning is drawn out of the river. What could be better? Exact to your cue, dead or alive, at least you've given them the opportunity of keeping up the legend. Accident? – well, perhaps! they'll say. Heart failure? – maybe! Poor Mrs Greville, everybody knows how she adored that husband of hers – she died because she couldn't live without him!'

More Compelling Fiction from Headline

EDITH PARGETER

She goes to War

It is 1940. Catherine Saxon is on her way to join the Women's Royal Naval Service at its Quarters in Devonport. She isn't quite sure why she joined up in the first place. A journalist on a local paper, her brief had been to cover gossip and fashion, so she was hardly in the front line! But join up she did, and her impulsive decision is to have undreamt-of consequences...

Sent first for basic training as a teleprinter operator, Catherine is surprised to find she enjoys the camaraderie of her fellow WRNS and quickly grows to love the beautiful Devon countryside. A posting to Liverpool comes as something of a shock, but she soon acclimatises to the war-torn city, and it is here, one fine day in early spring, that she meets the man who is to have such a profound effect on her life.

Tom Lyddon is a veteran of the Spanish Civil War and his political beliefs strike an immediate chord with Catherine. In wartime, the usual stages of courtship are dispensed with, and she readily accepts Tom's invitation to spend a few days with him in the blissful solitude of the North Wales countryside. Their idyll ends when Tom is recalled to active service abroad, and then all Catherine can do is wait – and hope – for her lover's safe return...

Also by Edith Pargeter from Headline
The Brothers of Gwynedd Quartet, The Eighth Champion of Christendom,
Reluctant Odyssey, Warfare Accomplished,
and, writing as Ellis Peters,
A Rare Benedictine, The Hermit of Eyton Forest, The Confession of Brother
Haluin, The Heretic's Apprentice, The Summer of the Danes, The Holy Thief,
Brother Cadfael's Penance, City of Gold and Shadows, Death Mask, Death to the
Landlords, Flight of the Witch, Holiday with Violence, Mourning Raga, Never Pick
up Hitch-hikers, The Assize of the Dying, Funeral of Figaro, The Horn of Roland,
The Piper on the Mountain, The Will and the Deed

FICTION/GENERAL   0 7472 3277 6

A selection of bestsellers from Headline

APPOINTED TO DIE	Kate Charles	£4.99 ☐
SIX FOOT UNDER	Katherine John	£4.99 ☐
TAKEOUT DOUBLE	Susan Moody	£4.99 ☐
POISON FOR THE PRINCE	Elizabeth Eyre	£4.99 ☐
THE HORSE YOU CAME IN ON	Martha Grimes	£5.99 ☐
DEADLY ADMIRER	Christine Green	£4.99 ☐
A SUDDEN FEARFUL DEATH	Anne Perry	£5.99 ☐
THE ASSASSIN IN THE GREENWOOD	P C Doherty	£4.99 ☐
KATWALK	Karen Kijewski	£4.50 ☐
THE ENVY OF THE STRANGER	Caroline Graham	£4.99 ☐
WHERE OLD BONES LIE	Ann Granger	£4.99 ☐
BONE IDLE	Staynes & Storey	£4.99 ☐
MISSING PERSON	Frances Ferguson	£4.99 ☐

All Headline books are available at your local bookshop or newsagent, or can be ordered direct from the publisher. Just tick the titles you want and fill in the form below. Prices and availability subject to change without notice.

Headline Book Publishing, Cash Sales Department, Bookpoint, 39 Milton Park, Abingdon, OXON, OX14 4TD, UK. If you have a credit card you may order by telephone – 0235 400400.

Please enclose a cheque or postal order made payable to Bookpoint Ltd to the value of the cover price and allow the following for postage and packing:
UK & BFPO: £1.00 for the first book, 50p for the second book and 30p for each additional book ordered up to a maximum charge of £3.00.
OVERSEAS & EIRE: £2.00 for the first book, £1.00 for the second book and 50p for each additional book.

Name ....

Address ....

....

....

If you would prefer to pay by credit card, please complete:
Please debit my Visa/Access/Diner's Card/American Express (delete as applicable) card no:

Signature .... Expiry Date ....